Changing Light

A Wentworth Cove Novel: Book 2

Rebecca Stevenson

Copyright © 2015 Rebecca Stevenson

All rights reserved.

ISBN: 1517530288
ISBN-13: 978-1517530280

Dedication

To the memory of Carlin Marie Ascher,
who lived life with love and joy,
viewed the changing light with dignity and grace,
and dances in a brighter light now

Contents

Chapter One	1
Chapter Two	10
Chapter Three	19
Chapter Four	25
Chapter Five	31
Chapter Six	40
Chapter Seven	47
Chapter Eight	52
Chapter Nine	57
Chapter Ten	66
Chapter Eleven	71
Chapter Twelve	82
Chapter Thirteen	88
Chapter Fourteen	97
Chapter Fifteen	108
Chapter Sixteen	116
Chapter Seventeen	122

Chapter Eighteen	131
Chapter Nineteen	136
Chapter Twenty	143
Chapter Twenty-One	150
Chapter Twenty-Two	154
Chapter Twenty-Three	163
Chapter Twenty-Four	170
Chapter Twenty-Five	175
Chapter Twenty-Six	184
Chapter Twenty-Seven	193
Chapter Twenty-Eight	200
Chapter Twenty-Nine	208
Chapter Thirty	214
Chapter Thirty-One	220
About the Author	226

Chapter One

On a cool, crisp Saturday morning in July, Faith Parker opened her eyes slightly and peeked at her phone to check the time. The enticing thought of closing her eyes and rolling back over crept across her mind. After all, she'd have to get up early soon enough. But she'd borrowed a school key for today and was eager to get her new kindergarten classroom ready for the first day of school. She eased out of bed and tentatively put her feet on the cold hardwood floor.

But first things first. Wrapping herself in her fluffy pink robe, she headed for the kitchen, hoping someone had already brewed a pot of coffee. She smelled it before opening the kitchen door and smiled at the thought of curling her cold fingers around a warm mug. After pouring an extra large portion of her morning addiction, she started back to her bedroom to dress for the first visit to her new school in Kennebunk, Maine.

"Daniel!" Faith called to her brother as she pulled a sweater over her blouse. Although she liked the autumn feel of New England's summer weather, she was still trying to get used to it after so many years of triple digits in Texas. Clouds hung low and crowded out the rising sun, and there was a real nip in the air. She thought it wouldn't take long to get used to it...but wondered what December and January would bring.

Faith didn't believe in coincidence—providence maybe, but not coincidence—so when her dad accepted the position of minister at Wentworth Cove Community Church and there was an opening in the Kennebunk Elementary School for a kindergarten teacher, she felt she should move with her parents and eleven-year-old brother Daniel, although she'd just graduated from Texas A&M and was eager to live on her own. She'd try it for a year or two anyway. Her parents' delight was surpassed only by Daniel's.

Trent Abramson was less enthusiastic about the move. He and Faith had dated during their senior year at Texas A&M, and he'd hinted on more than one occasion that there might be a ring in the future. Faith wasn't sure how she felt about that. Trent seemed perfect on paper: a finance major who no doubt had a bright and lucrative future, easy on the eyes—at least that's how her girlfriends described him—and totally devoted to her. Before they graduated, Trent had received and accepted a job offer with a bank in Dallas, and since Faith and her family lived there, he fully expected their relationship to continue without interruption. Only time would tell what the future held now that she lived almost two thousand miles away, but Faith knew that if she and Trent were meant to be together, distance wouldn't change anything about their feelings for one another. He, on the other hand, wasn't as optimistic.

Faith could understand his concern but continued to assure him that "if it's meant to be, it will be," so they agreed to stay in touch at least once or twice a week, and if either wanted to date someone else, they would.

Now that Faith was making Wentworth Cove her home, for the time being anyway, she couldn't wait to start her new life as a kindergarten teacher. It's what she'd dreamed of doing since she could remember. As a child, she would line up her dolls and "teach" them how to read. Her list to Santa when she was nine included a white marker board and a box of six dry-erase markers. Each color would represent a different subject, she told her mom. That would keep their interest, she'd said, for surely they loved bright colors. One of the first things she'd bought after receiving a call from the principal of Kennebunk Elementary School offering her a position as kindergarten teacher was a variety pack of six dry-erase markers—a different color for each subject—and she couldn't wait to start using them.

Daniel wiped sleep from his eyes. "What?" he managed to squeak after a few seconds.

"Want to go with me to the school and help me start decorating my room?"

"Sure. Why not? There's nothing else to do around here."

Faith understood Daniel's boredom. She didn't share it, but she understood it and wanted to keep him occupied until he could meet some boys his age, as much as, if not more than, she needed help decorating her classroom. In truth, she'd rather work by herself. This was a major part of teaching kindergarten she'd been waiting for—putting up posters, decorating bulletin boards, arranging desks and tables, setting up learning centers. She felt as called to creating a welcoming environment as to teaching a room full of five-year-olds how to read. *After all*, she rationalized, *they'll feel better about coming into a strange room if it's pretty and has a warm, inviting feel.*

Faith anticipated lots of tears and fears from her students on the first day, for she'd been one of those kindergartners who felt safer at home with her mother and didn't like getting out of her comfort zone. She hoped she could help calm their fears as well as her kindergarten teacher, Mrs. Williams, had calmed hers.

"You might need a light jacket over your T-shirt. It's in the sixties out there today," she told her brother.

"Nah. I'll be fine. I'm not a wuss, Faith."

Faith had to smile. Her little brother kept her life interesting. "You're not, huh? I had no idea…"

"Daniel, I'll be back in an hour or so," Emily Parker called to her son. "I'm going to run this chicken spaghetti over to Mrs. Norsworthy. She's the lady who got out of the hospital yesterday. You probably remember her as 'The Cake Lady.'" Kate Norsworthy was the first person Emily had met when she and her family moved from Dallas to Wentworth Cove, Maine.

A long-time member of Wentworth Cove Community Church's congregation, Kate had made it a point to call on the Parkers and see if they needed anything while they were moving in. This kindness, along with her Italian cream cake, had won over the whole family, especially Daniel, who managed to eat well over his fourth of the welcome offering.

"If you need anything before I get back, call Dad at the church office. The number's by the phone. And Faith will be back soon."

"I'll be fine," Daniel assured his mom. "I'm going to school with Faith anyway to help her get her room ready…Wait! Chicken spaghetti? Did you keep enough for us?" Emily laughed. She'd often thought her eleven-year-old son must have a tapeworm. "Hey, would you ask her if she knows anybody my age here? I can't wait for school to

At first she thought if she moved he might break, but she quickly got the hang of it and took to being a big sister as easily as Daniel took to being held all the time. As they grew older, the closeness remained. When Faith started driving, she hauled him around anywhere he wanted to go. As an eleven-year-old boy, he tried to act cool, but when he found out Faith would be moving with the family to Wentworth Cove, he had let out a squeal that likely could be heard throughout their Dallas neighborhood.

Emily didn't see a doorbell, so she knocked lightly on Kate Norsworthy's door. "Kate? It's Emily Parker."

"Come in, Emily. The door's unlocked."

Emily entered the living room of Kate's pale blue, white-shuttered cottage and thought about how different houses were in Wentworth Cove. Each one seemed to ooze with history and have a distinct personality. Some even had names. Kate's was especially inviting with red and white petunias lining the curved stone walkway to the door and window boxes full to overflowing with white trailing geraniums.

"Probably seems like a strange custom to you, doesn't it?" Kate continued. "Leaving our doors unlocked?"

"It does. I haven't felt the need to lock our door here, but I can't seem to get out of the habit." Emily was always willing—and even happy—to go where Andy was called, but this time she wondered how long it would take to get used to small-town living. Or if she *ever* could.

"Sit down, Emily. Can I get you a cup of coffee?" Kate Norsworthy, Emily observed, was an attractive woman whose looks belied her age. She had a teenage granddaughter, but except for her salt-and-pepper hair, which today she wore pulled back and tied with a white ribbon at the nape of her neck, Kate Norsworthy could

start. You know…not the homework, but…do tl
recess in sixth grade?"

"Never thought I'd hear you say you can't ⟨
school to start. You bored already?"

"A little," he confessed. "It's not like I can ride ɪ
over to Mitch's house or call Trevor to meet me
gym and shoot hoops. Every time we move I have tᴏ
some new guys."

"I know, honey, but it never takes you long to
new friends. You've always taken the moves better
Faith. Didn't you meet Mitch the first Sunday aftᴇ
moved last time?"

"Yeah."

"And you'll probably meet someone here soon,
But I'll ask Mrs. Norsworthy if she knows anyone."

Of Emily's two children, Daniel had always been
one she didn't have to worry about. Outgoing ɑ
gregarious, he was usually surrounded by people—and ɪ
only people his age. He was able somehow to cut acrᴏ
age barriers. Young and old, male and female—everybo
liked Daniel. Emily would have thought it was because
was a minister's son and had had the run of the church…
it hadn't been for Faith. But Faith had grown up in thos
same surroundings, and although she and Daniel weɪ
close—closer than one would expect for siblings mor
than a decade apart in age—she was Emily's quiet
introspective child. *At twenty-two, no longer a child*, Emily
thought, making a mental correction. *Faith might not make
friends as quickly as Daniel does, but still waters run deep.*

This move had worried Emily the most where her
daughter was concerned. They were a close family, and
Emily and Andy loved having Faith back home after four
years. Daniel didn't talk about it, but he had missed her
greatly, too. Eleven years old when he was born, Faith had
treated Daniel like a china doll, acting like a proud and
protective mother hen from the moment her mother had
gingerly laid him in her outstretched little-girl arms.

pass for someone in her forties. Her soft, unwrinkled olive skin and light gray-green eyes added to her youthful look.

"No. I don't want to trouble you. I just brought over some chicken spaghetti and a salad and hoped it would help a little until you can get back on your feet. I've heard about what a good cook you are and we enjoyed your scrumptious cake, so I'm sure it won't hold a candle to your cooking."

"Thank you. I know I'll enjoy it immensely. Would you mind putting it in the refrigerator for me? The kitchen is through the door on the right."

"Of course." Emily put the meal in Kate's refrigerator, let her eyes sweep the immaculate kitchen decorated in French country style, and went back to the living room where Kate remained seated on an overstuffed floral loveseat with her feet up on a matching hassock.

"How are you feeling today? I'm sorry I didn't get to the hospital to see you. It's no excuse, but we're still living around boxes, and I'm trying to tackle them one at a time so that I can at least start out organized. You'd think I'd have this moving thing down by now."

"Much better now that I'm home. I slept through the night for the first time in a week. It's awfully hard to sleep in a hospital, you know. If they're not waking you to take your temperature and blood pressure, they're putting ice in the water pitcher at four in the morning. That night crew needs something to do, I guess. Please don't feel bad about not visiting. I really didn't feel like having company in the hospital anyway."

"That's true about not getting any rest in a hospital. Ironic, isn't it?" Emily smiled, her eyes lighting up her face. "Is there anything I can do for you before I go? I'm sure you're not supposed to lift anything heavy. Could I take out your trash, put on a load of laundry, or do anything else to help?"

"Thank you, but my two sons have been hovering, actually. I had to run Nathan off this morning. He came over and made my breakfast and did a couple of handyman things. I'm so fortunate to have them both close. Have you met my new daughter-in-law?"

"I don't think so, but I've been trying to remember the names of everyone at WCCC. It's a daunting task."

"I suppose it would be, at that. Tracy's a dear. She and my younger son Nathan met when she came for a month last year and rented a cottage two doors down from me. I can't exactly claim responsibility for the match, but I was overjoyed about it. They were married about a month before you and Reverend Parker moved here. In fact, they live, temporarily anyway, in the cottage she rented last summer."

"You're fortunate to have them close," Emily said, thinking of how happy she'd been when Faith decided to come to Maine.

"I am. She's a literary agent at a firm in Boston, but she finally convinced her boss that everything is done electronically anyway."

"Isn't that the truth? What would we do without our cell phones and computers? I'm glad they were able to work that out. Well, I'll be on my way, but I trust you to call if there's anything I can do. Take care of yourself." Emily started out the door, remembered Daniel's request and turned. "Oh. I almost forgot. My son, Daniel, wanted me to ask if you know anyone his age in Wentworth Cove. He's usually so outgoing and makes friends easily, but he hasn't met anyone yet. I guess there aren't many eleven-year-old boys here. He might have to wait until school starts."

"Hmmm... Let me think on that. Nathan volunteers at a YMCA day camp. He might have a suggestion. Does Daniel have any special interests?"

"He's just a normal boy...whatever that is these days. Rides his bike, plays a little basketball, likes a few video games. He's developing an interest in photography. His sister gave him a camera for Christmas and he's been taking pictures everywhere he goes. He wants to learn how to do more...how to use all the gadgets, I think."

"That does give me an idea. Let me make a call and get back to you. You leave Daniel to me. I need a new project now that Nathan and Tracy's wedding is over."

Chapter Two

When Faith Parker had first seen the sea and tasted the sweet salt air of Wentworth Cove, she knew she'd made the right decision to come to Maine. Having been landlocked in Texas for most of her twenty-two years, her only exposure to water consisted of a few rivers and lakes. She'd seen sailboats on White Rock Lake in Dallas, but they couldn't compare with the full-masted schooners that skimmed the surface of the Atlantic well beyond the rocks and sand of the Maine coast. Even the lobster boats, proud, old, and beautiful in their own way, captivated her.

She'd camped out with friends and rafted down the Brazos River a couple of times, but the Brazos didn't come close to the majesty of the Atlantic as she watched waves crashing against those craggy rocks when the tide came in.

When the sky was just the right shade, it was hard to tell where it ended and the sea began. Sometimes the only signs of a faint horizon were the occasional sailboats that floated by in the distance. Faith was especially taken with the boats with bright-colored sails and yearned for the day when she would be on a sailboat heading for that fine, almost invisible line where the sea meets the sky.

The drive from Wentworth Cove to Kennebunk differed so much different from what Faith was accustomed to. No freeways. No four-lane avenues with wide tree-lined medians. Simply two-lane, meandering roads for the most part. But picturesque, she had to admit. *I'll give up big highways and wide-open spaces for this kind of beauty any day.* The cooler summer temperatures and frequent rains ensured the growth of vegetation, and she thought she'd never seen so many blue, lavender, and pink hydrangeas in her life.

"Faith...Hey, Faith . . ." She realized she was in a daze and Daniel was talking to her.

"Yeah. What?"

"What were you thinking about? It's like you were totally zoned out or something."

"Yeah. Well. I was just thinking about how different Maine is from Texas."

"Are you sorry you came with us?"

"No. Not at all. I like it. It's just going to take some getting used to. That's all. What about you? Do you like it here?"

"I don't think so," Daniel confessed. He added quickly, "But don't tell Dad. He likes the new church, and I don't want to make him sad."

"You're a great brother, you know that, kiddo? There aren't many guys your age who'd be so thoughtful of their parents that way." Faith had always thought her little brother special, but the more time she spent with him, the more she realized he was indeed a cut above most eleven-year-olds. What other boy his age would be so concerned about his dad's feelings?

"I won't tell him, but why don't you like it here? Is it just too different from what you've always been used to?"

"Well..." Daniel pondered how best to answer the question. "I like the ocean and all. It's cool. And I don't really want school to start soon... I mean, I'm happy for you. You're excited about it. But, you know, I heard sixth grade is a lot harder than fifth grade, so I'm not excited about all the homework and stuff like that. But there's nothing to do here."

"You're helping me decorate my classroom, aren't you?" *But what fifth grade boy wants to decorate a kindergarten classroom on a summer day? He must be* really *bored.* "I know you'd rather be playing with your friends back home, buddy. Have you heard from Mitch lately?"

"No. He probably goes to the Y with Luke and Trevor every day."

"Well, thanks for helping me today. I didn't want to have to do this by myself. I see you brought your camera. Planning on some 'before and after' shots?"

"I thought you'd like some pictures of your bulletin boards so next year when you put them up you'll remember what you did this year."

Faith had to smile at this. Why hadn't she thought of it? *Little brother, you're pretty awesome.*

"That's a great idea, Daniel. And I'm going to think of some other things for you to do until school starts. That'll be my mission after I get my room ready."

Kate Norsworthy was on a mission, too. She had an idea, and it involved her son David's art gallery. Thinking her granddaughter might play accomplice in her plan, she picked up her phone and dialed Jessica's number.

"Hey, Jess. How's everything at the gallery today? I'm sorry I can't relieve you for lunch. Maybe in a couple of days I'll feel up to it."

"Oh, Gram. That's the last thing you should be worrying about now. Take it easy for a while. Besides, we're fine. Tim's picking up lunch from Lobster Bistro, and we'll take turns eating, so there'll always be someone in the gallery. How are you feeling?"

Jessica Norsworthy and Tim Grayson had dated for over a year. Tim would soon be heading to the prestigious Bowdoin College less than an hour away in Brunswick, Maine, but Jessica had one more year of high school before she could join him. At least she *hoped* to join him there. Tim had won a full academic scholarship, and that would be the only way she could attend Bowdoin, but she was determined. It would give her something to work toward while missing Tim. And he would come home every weekend. They could make it work. She was sure of that.

"Oh, I'm fine," Kate answered her granddaughter. "Glad to be home. I'm calling about that photographer who's having a showing at the gallery in a couple of weeks. I met him the other day when he brought some photographs by. I think his name's Josh. Don't remember his last name, though. Do you know how I could get in touch with him?"

"Now what do you have up your sleeve days after major surgery? Matchmaking would be my guess, but I can't imagine with whom. Is there someone new in Wentworth Cove this summer that I haven't met? You've run out of sons, so now you're resorting to people you've met only once?"

"Such impertinence from my favorite granddaughter," Kate quipped.

"Your *only* granddaughter," Jessica returned. "Anyway, you're in luck. His name is Josh Whitehall, and he'll be in this afternoon. He's bringing more framed photos for the show next month. They're amazing. I hope we have a good turnout since this is our first one-man show featuring a photographer. When Dad saw his work, he jumped at a chance to showcase him."

"Well, here's what I have up my sleeve, as you say. Have you met the new minister, Reverend Parker?"

"Yeah."

"His wife came by this morning...brought a casserole...and said her son hasn't met anyone his age since they moved here. He's eleven, so a little older than the kids Nathan works with, but she also said he's interested in photography, so—"

"So you *are* matchmaking again, just in a different way this time. But this time you're working on *two* new people, not just one." Jessica had to laugh. "This is so like you, Gram, trying to make everyone's life better. And if a little interfering on your part is needed, well, so much the better."

"I'm hopeless, aren't I?"

"I wouldn't want my grandmother to be one bit different. You want me to ask if he'll take the boy under wing and mentor him...or just give him some tips about talking pictures? Do you know what kind of camera he has?"

"I have no idea, but yes. Would you do that? See if he has time. I don't want him to think he owes us just because your dad is giving him his first one-man show, but—"

"But it *is* a good opportunity for him, right, and if he's like the local artists we've showcased here, he'll seriously sell some photos, so—"

"Exactly. I'm not at all beyond putting a guilt trip on him to help a little boy."

"Sure, Gram. I'll go along with your little scheme. I'll call you as soon as he leaves."

Josh Whitehall's black Jeep crunched over the gravel in the small parking lot of Norsworthy Art Gallery and rolled to a stop under the shade of a red oak tree. Jessica watched him through the front window, her eyes wide at the appearance of this young man who could pass for a

California surfer more easily than a Maine photographer. His longish, sandy blond hair kept falling over his ice-blue eyes but was back in place with a slight flick of his head. His face was clean-shaven and tan, his body lean and strong.

As Josh trudged up the gallery steps carrying a box full of framed photographs, Jessica snapped back to reality, jumped up, and rushed to open the front door for him.

"Thanks...Jessica, right?"

"Good memory. Dad's not here right now, but he said to put these upstairs in the closet with the others."

"Will do."

Josh deposited his wares and turned to go back down to the main gallery, but hesitated when he saw an open door beckoning him to a deck. His ever-present curiosity drew him to the door and beyond. After taking two steps outside and seeing the magnificent view, he chided himself for not having his camera. He could go back to the car and retrieve it, or he could whip out his phone for now and bring the Nikon in the next time he came with another box of photos. He snapped a couple of quick shots and determined to come back in a day or two, telephoto lens in hand, in time for a sunset photo opportunity.

"Everything okay?" Jessica asked when he returned.

"Oh, sure. I saw the deck and had to take some shots. It's what I do." He winked and revealed a crooked grin that exhibited a hint of mischief.

"I understand. You're not the first to capture that scenery. That's a deck with quite a history, too."

"Yeah? What do you mean?"

"My uncle Nathan met his wife on that deck last summer, and they've been married for a month. Also, that's where I got my first kiss," Jessica continued with a glint in her eye. "You never know what might happen up there."

"You're not old enough to be kissing boys," Josh teased.

"Ouch."

"I don't think my activities today will contribute to its historical significance. I'll see you in a couple of days with more framed photos. By the way, I'm needing to grab a quick bite to eat before I head back to Portland. Any chance I could get lucky in Wentworth Cove? Lobster rolls? Crab cakes? Heck, at this point I'd even settle for a burger."

"My boyfriend—yes, I'm old enough—is picking up lunch from Lobster Bistro today. I could call him and tell him to pick up something for you, too."

"No. That's okay. I'll eat there if you'll tell me where it is. Duty calls."

"Turn right at the first stop sign on the way back to Portland. It's about a block and a half down on the right. Not much parking so if you want to leave your Jeep parked here and walk…"

"I think I'll do tha—"

"Oh! I almost forgot. My grandmother wanted me to ask you something. Do you have another minute?"

"I'm pretty hungry." He winked. "Just kidding. What is it?"

"Well, it seems there's this new kid in town. I think he's eleven. He's interested in photography and hasn't met anyone his age since he moved here. She was wondering if you would meet him and give him some pointers about how to use his camera. You'd have to know my grandmother to fully understand this. Her life's goal is to make sure everyone in Wentworth Cove is happy."

"A worthy goal, I'm sure, but I don't think everyone was born to be happy. I hate to disappoint her, but I really don't like kids. You're the exception, of course." And he winked again.

"Very funny. I'll tell her. You're right. She *will* be disappointed, and this might not be the last you hear of this. Just saying."

"If you all feel like I owe—"

"It's definitely not that. In fact, my mom and dad don't know anything about this. It's all Gram. I told her I'd throw it out there. If you don't feel comfortable—" Jessica started. "No. You shouldn't feel obligated at all. My dad is happy to be showcasing your work. He thinks you're an awesome photographer. Don't give this another thought. I'll explain to Gram."

Why are there always kids involved? Josh thought as he walked up the cracked stone path to Lobster Bistro. *I get a golden opportunity to jumpstart my photography career with a great one-man show at an art gallery, and someone has to ask me to take on a kid and teach him how to use his camera. Whatever happened to reading the instructions? That's how I learned. He can do that, too. I can't feel guilty for saying no. I won't feel guilty.*

"Hi. Table for one?" Annie Culwell surveyed the stranger who had just walked into Lobster Bistro. Eyed him up and down, her green eyes finally resting on his clear blue ones.

"Yes."

She led him to a booth in the corner of the restaurant, passing many empty booths and tables.

"Are you here for the summer?"

"Just the day...well, half day, actually. Heading back to Portland after I eat."

"You're from Portland? I *love* Portland."

"Yeah?"

"Any place is better than Wentworth Cove. I'd rather live in Boston, but Portland's a pretty cool town, too."

"Do you think I could get a menu?"

"Oh yeah. Sure. Here."

"I don't mean to be rude, but I need to get back to work soon."

"What do you do?"

"I'm a photographer."

"Oh. Wow. A photographer from Portland. Oh sorry. I'll let you look at the menu. We have great lobster rolls here. Back in a minute to take your order."

"I'll take a cheeseburger with everything. No mayo. Lots of mustard."

"That was fast. I like a guy who knows what he wants."

"What I want right now is to eat and get back to work."

"Sure. I'll go put in the order. Shouldn't take long. We're not as busy as usual. Oh, my name is Annie, by the way. Annie Culwell. Let me know if you need anything else. Anything." A slight smile traveled across her face, and the look in her eyes told Josh she meant it. This Annie Culwell was offering him more than what was on the menu at Lobster Bistro.

When she came back to his booth with a burger and fries, he asked, "How old are you, Annie Culwell?"

"Nineteen. I graduated from high school a year ago and plan to go to college in the fall."

"Well, that's great. I wish you luck."

Annie took his hand and wrote her phone number with a ballpoint pen on his left palm. "Don't wash that hand."

"A carryover from high school? No one's done that to me since I was in the tenth grade."

"It doesn't matter. Still works for me. Call me sometime, and you won't regret it."

Josh was amused. She was cute, wore a little too much makeup for his taste, but he hadn't had a date in a while. He doubted he'd call her, but he wasn't dating anyone else, so what the heck? She was a little young, but not as young as Jessica…in many ways.

Chapter Three

Remembering he'd left his Jeep at the art gallery, Josh headed back in that direction. As he walked, he looked around noting the beauty of this small town he'd only recently discovered. Originally from Boston, Josh had moved to Portland after college to pursue a career in photography, much to the displeasure of his attorney parents, who thought he would go to law school and join them in the family practice. Josh had never cared to follow in his parents' footsteps, but to appease them he'd majored in pre-law. With graduation approaching, however, it was time to start applying to law schools. But he realized he couldn't follow through with it, so he cut and ran, found a magazine in Portland looking for a photographer, and began making a life there.

His father had exploded. "Do you realize how much it costs to put someone through Harvard? Why would you let us pay an exorbitant amount for a four-year degree you never planned to use? What exactly is it you do now? Take pictures? Anyone can do that without a Harvard degree.

Just point and shoot. What were you thinking, son? If you're thinking at all, that is."

"So you're still calling me your son? I don't feel like your son. A son would be treated with more respect. If you really cared, you'd try to understand that I'm not a younger version of you. I majored in pre-law to make you happy. It didn't make me happy. I tried to please you. To do what I knew you and Mother wanted me to do, but it's not me. I'm not cut out to be a lawyer. I can't imagine putting on a suit every day and going to an office. I can't imagine standing before a judge or jury arguing for something or someone I might or might not believe in. Why can't you understand that? Why can't you see me for who I am? I'm sorry you're disappointed, but I have to do what makes me happy. I have to at least try to make it on my own."

"Well, that's just what you'll be doing...making it on your own. Don't expect any help from us. We've done all we're going to do. Good luck. I love you, son, but I am disappointed. I won't sugarcoat it. Mother and I are both disappointed."

"I know I've disappointed you in many ways—"

"Joshua, what are you talking—"

"Dad, I know it, and there's nothing I can do about it. Nothing that would satisfy you. Nothing that would satisfy Mother. Nothing that would satisfy *me*. I can't change the past. God knows I've tried to in my mind so many times. But it is what it is, and no amount of wishing will change who I am or what I've done. What I failed to do. And no amount of wishing will bring Jordie back. I'm sorry. That's the best I can do. Bye, Dad."

"Son—"

And with that, Josh walked out of his Boston home and hadn't been back for two years. He'd spoken to his parents on a few occasions, like birthdays and Christmases, but he'd made a life for himself in Portland and was satisfied with it. He couldn't say he was completely happy.

He did miss his parents. They'd been good parents in their own country-club-crowd way. They'd raised him the way they'd been raised. Both of their fathers had been attorneys, and they had been expected to follow in their fathers' footsteps, which they'd both done.

But Josh was different. He hadn't inherited the attorney gene. He'd apparently inherited someone's recessive art gene. He felt like an artist when he was behind a camera. His talent was in knowing what to shoot, where to shoot, when to shoot, and editing his image to near perfection before printing or publishing. The magazine he worked for, *The Maine Way*, had been a perfect fit for him. His editor appreciated his work and gave him plenty of leeway with his assignments.

And he did regret the past he couldn't change. Walking out of his parents' house might have solved one problem, but Jordan Whitehall was never coming back, and Josh knew he alone was to blame. And neither time nor distance could ever change that.

When Josh got in his Jeep and noticed his Nikon on the passenger seat, he remembered the view from the upstairs deck of the art gallery. The sky was a bright cerulean dotted with fluffy, white clouds. The sun hid behind one of those clouds, the type of indirect light Josh preferred for shooting landscapes. He decided to go back in and get a couple of shots of the coast with his telephoto lens.

Jessica and Tim were finishing their lobster rolls when Josh opened the door.

"Hi, Josh. I didn't know you were coming back in. This is Tim Grayson. Tim, this is the photographer I told you about. His show is in a couple of weeks. Josh Whitehall."

"Tim," Josh said, sticking out his right hand.

"I'm happy to meet you. I've seen some of your photos. Hope you sell a lot."

"Thanks, man," Josh said and turned to Jessica. "I think I'll run back upstairs if you don't mind and get some shots before I head back to Portland. I hate to waste this perfect lighting."

"Sure. Just remember what I said about the deck. You never know," Jess retorted with a twinkle in her eye.

"You can count on me *not* to keep up that tradition."

Jessica, ever the romantic, fired back as Josh ascended the stairs, "Never say never."

Just then the door swung open and an exuberant Daniel Parker entered the gallery, almost in a run, followed by Faith. "Hi. I'm Daniel."

"Hello, Daniel. I'm Jessica and this is my friend Tim." Guessing this was the boy her grandmother was talking about, she said, "I see you have a camera. Want to take some cool photos while you're here?"

"You mean of these pictures?" Daniel asked skeptically, eyeing the framed oils, charcoals, pastels, and watercolors hanging on the walls.

"No. If you go up those stairs over there and go through the room, you'll see a door leading out to a deck. There's a really good view of the ocean from up there." Jessica decided she might as well help her Gram's plan along. Maybe when Josh met him, he'd have a harder time saying no.

"Cool," Daniel said, heading for the stairs. He stopped and turned to look at Faith. "Is that okay?"

"Sure, buddy. Go for it," Faith said, and Daniel bounded up the stairs. "Thanks for suggesting that. He's been bored since we moved here. He had so many friends in Dallas."

"Jess had an ulterior motive, which you'll know about pretty soon, I imagine," Tim said. "Jessica is her grandmother's protégée."

"Well, anything is appreciated. He's pretty special to me and I hate to see him unhappy. I came in to return your mother's school key. She brought it over the other night and I decorated my classroom today…that is, I got a good start. I can finish when in-service begins in a few weeks. Thank your mom for me, will you?"

"Sure."

"I'd better go up and get Daniel. I'm sure Mom still needs help unpacking the rest of our boxes, and this is the day Dad sequesters himself in his study to polish his sermon."

"That camera is *sweet*! Hi, I'm Daniel."

"Thanks. I was just leaving. The deck is all yours." *Oh great*, Josh thought. *This must be the boy Jessica was talking about.*

"Is that a telephoto lens?"

"Yeah. I'll get out of your way now so you can get some good shots."

"You're not in the way. I was just wondering if you're using a filter. I have one, but I've never tried it."

"I don't usually use a filter. I do edit before I print, though."

"My sister gave me this camera for Christmas. She's downstairs talking to Jessica and Tim. Jessica told me about the view up here and told me it was a good place to get pictures of the ocean. Do you take pictures from here often?"

Ambushed! Just wait until I have a talk with Miss Jessica Norsworthy.

Faith was good at reading people, and she read *disgust* all over Josh's face when she walked onto the deck. Whoever this guy was, he obviously didn't want to be bothered by a boy with a camera. "I'm sorry. My brother is interested in learning more about photography, but we don't want to take up your time if you were about to leave."

"I have to get back to work." But as Josh was turning to go, something magnet-like was pulling him to stay. Or was it a *someone*? He'd had lots of girlfriends, but this girl was different. Was that a Southern accent he recognized in her lilting voice? She didn't sound like most of the girls he knew. Didn't look like them either, with that auburn hair cascading in soft waves halfway down her back and a sprinkling of freckles across her nose. In fact, there was a softness about her he'd never seen in a girl. And when she brushed past him to stand by Daniel, why did she have to smell like spring flowers?

After a few seconds of self-talk, he rushed back into the room and down the stairs. He didn't have time or inclination to talk to a pesky little boy about his camera. This must be the one Jessica was talking about, he surmised, and he'd already told her he wasn't interested in taking on this project. But why did the kid have to have such a hot sister?

Chapter Four

"We're gonna need a bigger gallery!" David Norsworthy said to his brother Nathan, surveying the room, obviously happy with the turnout. It seemed the entire town showed up for Josh Whitehall's one-man show.

"He is talented, isn't he? I love the way he captures the area. In fact, I think I'll use him to do my cover shot when I publish that Great American Novel I'm working on."

"You haven't said anything about it in a while. How's it coming?"

"I finally let Tracy read it, with the caveat that she definitely will not represent me…even if she loved it, which she did, of course. I'm working on a few last-minute revisions she suggested. It doesn't hurt to be married to a literary agent. I refuse to use any of her contacts, though. Just her suggestions with the pacing of the plot. I'm going to start querying other agents, and maybe a few small presses, soon. Fingers crossed."

"How long have you known me, Nathan?"

"Is that a trick question, David? Uh. Let's see. About thirty-one years, if memory serves. Why?"

"And how long have you known Tracy?"

"What are you getting at, bro?"

"Just wondering why she gets to read your masterpiece before I do. And here I thought I was your favorite brother."

"You know how private I am about my writing, but if you really want to, I'll email the manuscript to you. That is, if you promise to give me a totally honest evaluation after you read it."

"When have I ever not been honest with you? Brutally honest at times, in fact. Remember that time you dated that Wendy Graham? Did I hold back on telling you what I thought of her?"

"Ouch. You could have gone a few more years without mentioning her again. Thank goodness I got that one out of my system."

"Anyway, send your manuscript to me. I'll make confetti out of it if I don't like it. And that's a promise, little brother."

"Deal."

"I need to work the room. Want to walk around with me and greet guests? It looks like I've left Elizabeth and Jessica to do all the work."

"I think I'll find Tracy and take advantage of some of that free food across the room. I'm really happy about this great turnout, Dave."

"Thanks. Just hope Josh sells a lot of photos and the gallery gets some good exposure. Yeah, and before you can comment on it...no pun intended."

"None taken," Nathan quipped with a grin.

Josh Whitehall spotted Faith Parker the minute she and her family walked through the gallery door. They probably came, he surmised, because her little brother was into photography. But he hoped he could catch her away from

"No, my family likes to cook, so we don't eat out much. I don't think I've even tasted lobster, to be honest."

"Well, we'll have to do something about that. You can't live here and not know what lobster tastes like. How old are you?"

"I'm twenty-two. You?"

"Nineteen. I graduated from high school a year ago. I'm thinking about going to college in Boston…or getting a job and apartment in Portland after I save some money. Did you know Josh is from Portland? If I move there, I'm going to find out where he lives and try to move somewhere close so I'll know someone. He's pretty hot, don't you think?"

"Well, he seems nice, but I don't know him at all. We only met a few minutes ago."

"Do you have a boyfriend? You probably do, but my sister's thirty, and she doesn't, so…you never know."

"I do. But he lives in Texas. That's where I'm from."

"I don't know about a long-distance relationship. I don't think I'd like that. So is it working?"

"Well, I haven't lived here very long, you know, but we text a lot and FaceTime at least once a week. He's busy with a new job and I'll be working soon, but we're going to try to make it work."

"I can't believe you moved up here and left your boyfriend…where was it you came from?"

"Texas."

"You couldn't find a job down there?"

"I didn't try. I wanted to move here with my family."

"You did *not* just say that. I would move *away* from my family if I could. In fact, I plan to as soon as I can. I can't believe you gave up a guy to move to Wentworth Cove. Boring, isn't it? Aren't you sorry you came?"

"No. Not at all. It's been anything but boring. There's a lot to see here because it's so different from what I'm used to. And I've been spending some time getting my classroom ready."

"Oh. A teacher, huh? Hey! I just had an idea." Annie took out her phone. "Give me your number. I'll treat you to a lobster roll, and tell you about it. Do you have plans for Monday night?"

"No. That'll be nice. I haven't met anyone close to my age here…with the exception of Josh, but he doesn't count because I don't think we'll be hanging out."

"I plan to be hanging out with him, soon. Can't let one like that go."

Chapter Five

Emily Parker was the perfect minister's wife—laughing brown eyes, a voice that could soothe a savage beast, and a heart big enough to win over even the most cantankerous congregant…which she'd had to do more than once since marrying Andy Parker. Not that Andy himself had an adverse effect on his congregation, but she and Andy had been in the ministry together long enough for her to know that when Andy ruffled a few feathers along the way, she would have to come behind smoothing them back down in her quiet, unobtrusive way.

Andy Parker had been called to pastor the church when Reverend Brown had finally decided to retire. Charles Brown was loved by the entire community, and Andy knew he had big shoes to fill. At forty-five he was thirty years Charles's junior, but he hoped he could win over the people of this picturesque New England coastal village. What he couldn't accomplish, he felt sure his wife would be able to. He'd never met a soul who wasn't taken with Emily. Andy would visit the sick and lonely in his congregation and pray with them, but Emily would sit with them for hours on end, holding their hands, feeding them if they couldn't feed themselves, singing to them. She'd been a vocal music major in college, and although she had never had a career in which to use her degree, she'd put it to work for the benefit of others, singing solos in church and comforting those who were hurting. Andy couldn't imagine trying to do his job without her.

Emily picked up the phone on the second ring. "Mrs. Parker? It's Jessica Norsworthy from the art gallery."

"Hi, Jessica. How are you? I enjoyed the other day at the gallery when you were showcasing the photographer from Portland."

"I'm good. I was actually calling about that. Josh has agreed to meet with Daniel and give him some tips on photography. I don't know what changed his mind, but he called me this morning. Would Daniel still be interested?"

"I'm sure he would, Jessica." Emily hesitated. "But…how well do you know this Josh Whitehall? He's so talented, but I guess I could be called an overly protective mother. You really can't be too careful with your kids these days, you know?"

"Sure. Would you feel better if you talked with my gram? She got to know Josh pretty well while he was getting ready for the show. This whole thing about matching him up with Daniel was her plan anyway."

"That might be a good idea. Thanks. Is she there?"

"Just a minute. I'll get her."

While she was waiting to talk to Kate, Emily made her way back into the kitchen to stir the beef stew simmering on the stove. Add a salad and hot, buttered homemade bread, and it was one of her family's favorite meals, so she made it for them often.

"Emily? Hello. Jess says you're concerned about Josh Whitehall meeting with your son to give him some pointers on using his camera. I understand that."

"I'm glad you don't think I'm being over-reactive. I'd like Daniel to benefit from his knowledge, but it's hard for this mother hen to relinquish her little one to a stranger."

"Of course. I get it. Would it make you feel better if someone went with them? A chaperon of sorts?"

"It would, of course, but would that seem strange? I imagine I could talk Faith into it. She'd do just about anything for her little brother."

"Emily, I actually think this would be as good for Josh as it would for Daniel. There's a sadness behind that young man's eyes, and I don't know what's causing it. He's coming Saturday to pick up the photos that didn't sell. Will that work for Daniel and Faith?"

"I think so. Thanks for arranging this, Kate. I sometimes feel a little guilty about the times we've uprooted our kids and moved." She'd signed up for this when she became a minister's wife, but that didn't make it easier. She didn't mind it for herself, but Faith and Daniel, well…that was another matter.

"I think kids are pretty resilient, but I can understand your concern. I'll see if Saturday will work for Josh. An hour or so would be a good start, don't you think? I know the attention span of young boys these days. They can meet at the gallery. I don't know where else he'll want to take them."

"That's great. Faith will have him there. Just let me know the time."

Faith didn't know what was causing her excitement when she woke up Saturday morning, Daniel's exhilaration over having something fun to do for a change or her unexpected anticipation over seeing Josh again. But Josh wanted to capture the sunset, so she'd have to wait until seven o'clock, when they were set to meet at Norsworthy Art Gallery before heading for the beach.

Fortunately, the weather had warmed up from last weekend, so she could wear something other than jeans and a sweater. Shorts? Maybe not. A dress? They were going to the beach, but she didn't think a sundress would be wrong. In fact, the more she thought about it, the more she thought it was just the right touch, so she donned the white one with yellow flowers, cinching her waist with a lime green belt.

Faith was lost in thought when they arrived at the gallery, but as soon as she saw Josh's Jeep, she snapped back to reality. A little self-talk was in order, she decided. *It might be a good idea to think about Trent right now*, she told herself. *You don't know this guy. He volunteered to help Daniel and you're just along for the ride. That's it. Don't get caught up in that grin, those blue eyes, that charming fake Southern accent.*

Daniel bounced out of the car as soon as she rolled to a stop on the gravel parking area and was already talking to Josh when Faith walked in, so she wandered over to talk to Jessica.

"It's good of you to let us meet here."

"Norsworthy Art Gallery is the meeting place of record in Wentworth Cove, so it just makes sense." Jessica, Faith noted, was almost as outgoing and friendly as Daniel. Maybe the first person who could give him a run for his money in that area. "Did you get your classroom decorations finished?"

"Not quite finished, but I've made progress. It's a cute room already, so there's not much I have to do except put some more personal touches on it. I just need to finish a bulletin board and it'll be ready for the first day, I think."

Faith turned to Josh, and when Daniel stopped to take a breath, she said, "Did Mrs. Norsworthy tell you I'd be coming along, too? Don't get the wrong idea. It doesn't have anything to do with not trusting you specifically. My mom is just a little overprotective when it comes to her children. I'll stay out of the way while y'all are shooting."

Faith noticed that Josh was trying to suppress a grin and realized she'd slipped into her Texas lingo with that *y'all*. She'd vowed to break herself of that habit when she moved to New England. But old habits die hard, and every once in a while she slipped. She really didn't want to slip around Josh, though, because he'd take it and run with it.

"Sorry," she said. "I know how that must sound to everyone here. I'm trying to quit saying it, but it's hard, you know, when you've heard it all your life."

"Don't apologize. I know I teased you about it the last time we met, but if there's one thing I can't resist, it's a Southern accent."

Was Faith blushing? She felt she was and immediately changed the subject. "Should we go now? Do you want me to take my car?"

"No. Let's go in my Jeep. Yours looks squeaky clean. Mine's perpetually dirty from all the out-of-the-way places it has to take me. Plus, it has four-wheel drive, so it won't matter if we take it onto the beach."

Not being able to sit still while Faith and Josh were talking, Daniel had run upstairs to take some pictures off the deck again. "Daniel, are you ready to go?" Faith called.

"Yep. Coming."

Josh's Jeep rumbled down Harbor Road, turned onto Old Sea Pines, and finally made a left onto Shoreline Drive. Daniel had chatted the whole way from the backseat. Did Faith imagine it, or did Josh really usher her into the front on purpose? No, she decided. It meant nothing. He was being a gentleman to let her sit in the front. But in the back of her mind, she couldn't shake the suspicion that he wasn't very fond of Daniel. She knew he'd said no to Mrs. Norsworthy's idea initially.

But he did agree, so maybe she was wrong. She could hope she was anyway. For a guy as appealing as Josh Whitehall not to like Daniel Parker, he must have something wrong with him. Everyone was charmed by her little brother.

Josh parked the car on the shore and ran around to open the door for Faith. What were these mixed signals he was sending? The trip was for Daniel, but he seemed focused on her. She realized she was both flattered and angry. *If you're interested in me, be nice to my little brother because that goes a really long way with me.* Trent hadn't seemed very fond of Daniel, either, but she had to admit he wasn't around him much since she'd been away at college when she and Trent started dating.

Josh Whitehall? Interested in me? Who am I kidding? He doesn't know anything about me, and I'm just along because my parents wanted me to come. Get a grip, Faith. This trip is all about Daniel. But, on the other hand, why did he change his mind about giving Daniel photography tips right after we talked at the gallery?

"Hey, Josh." Daniel was ready to start the session. Ready to start doing something fun. "What are we going to shoot? Will you help me with my settings?"

"Sure. Just give me a minute to get my camera set up," Josh replied as he set the tripod in the wet sand of Wentworth Cove's shore. "Have you ever done any time lapse photography? That's what I'm going to do today."

"Time laps? Like laps you run?"

Josh smiled. "No. Time L-A-P-S-E. It means a passage of time. I set the shutter speed so that the lens will take in light for a few seconds. It works really well at night, especially when you want to capture the moon and stars, but I also use it to take pictures of water washing over the rocks on the beach."

"Oh. Cool."

"You know when you take a picture, and you hear the click of the shutter immediately? Well, I can set it for, say…three seconds, and it holds the shutter open for that long. Let me set mine up and take a couple of shots, and I'll show you what I mean. Meanwhile, why don't you show me what you can do with those shells on the sand over there?"

"Just focus and shoot?"

"Yeah. We'll start with that. What kind of an eye you have for composition. Don't get in too close, though, because you don't have a macro lens."

"What's a macro lens?"

"Don't worry about that right now. Just a lens you use to take really close-up shots. It's something we can get to later."

Faith had wandered off to force Josh to interact with Daniel and was shooting with her cell phone. Granted, she wouldn't get the same quality they would, but it kept her occupied while the guys bonded. At least she hoped Josh was warming up to Daniel. Because Daniel, she knew, was already crazy about Josh.

"Hey, Josh. Is it bad we're going to take pictures of the sunset today? Maybe we should come back when there aren't any clouds."

"Lesson number one, Daniel. Clouds make for more beautiful sunsets. Just wait and see. The cloud configuration tonight is going to be awesome for some sunset shots. Cloudless skies are boring at sunset. It's almost time, too. See. The sky is beginning to change color in the west. Pretty soon those colors will be more vibrant. Why don't we shoot some now and get some later as it changes."

"Cool. Where should my settings be?"

"Let me set them for now. Later we can get into the settings and the reasons for them."

"Hey, Faith. We're gonna get pics of the sunset. Wanna join us?" Daniel called to his sister, and she started back toward them. As she walked, her feet always just barely missing the rushing water, she couldn't help but notice a slight change in Josh. He was interacting with Daniel more. She had ceased to be amazed at the people her little brother could charm. And now it was apparent he was slowing winning over one Portland photographer.

"Let me see those shells you shot. How did they turn out?" Daniel handed Josh his camera.

"Hey, man. These are good. You have the eye of an artist."

"I do?" Daniel beamed with pride.

"Yeah. And they're focused perfectly. I think you have a future as a photographer."

"Well, I was thinking about being a professional basketball player, but if I don't grow tall enough, I could always be a photographer, right?"

"You could, bud. Okay. Get your camera ready to shoot this sunset. Why don't you take one or two shots every minute or so until the sun is completely below the horizon. And then a few minutes after that as the colors change and get even more pronounced. In a few days we can meet again, and I'll bring my laptop and show you how to edit them. Editing the photos is every bit as important as taking them."

"Sweet!"

They shot for about twenty minutes until it was time to go.

"One more thing," Josh said. "When you go on a sunset shoot, don't leave without turning around and looking behind you."

Daniel spun around in the sand. "Whoa! The whole sky is pink! Should I take a picture?"

"Go for it, bud," Josh said and Daniel started snapping. "The next time we meet I'll tell you about changing light and how important it is in photography."

"Changing light. Okay. Can Faith come with us again?"

"Sure she can," Josh replied, cutting his eyes over to Daniel's sister and smiling.

Chapter Six

Emily Parker opened the door of her husband's home office and tentatively stuck her head in. He usually didn't like to be interrupted when he was beginning preparation for Sunday's sermon, but his wife was always welcome. She didn't interrupt him much and when she did, he knew it was important...to her anyway. "Andy, what do you know about this Josh guy?"

"This *what* guy?" Andy mentally ran through the names he could remember of the members of his new congregation, but *Josh* didn't ring a bell.

"Josh. You know. The one who had the photo event at the gallery and offered to show Daniel some things about the camera? Don't get me wrong. I'm happy Daniel has something to do and he's really excited about it, but what do you know about him?"

"Isn't Faith with them?"

"Yeah."

"But you're still worried about your little chick, mama hen? Or are you worried about *both* of your chicks? He and Faith appear to be about the same age. Is that it?" Andy closed his Bible and his laptop and motioned for his wife to sit on the sofa across the room. He joined her there. If this was something important enough for Emily to interrupt sermon preparation, it was important enough for him to give her his full attention.

"Of course not. Faith can take care of herself. Besides she's practically engaged to Trent. You just can't be too careful these days. I know you always think the best of people, but sometimes they aren't who you'd like them to be and you're just fooling yourself."

Andy wasn't as sure as Emily seemed to be that Faith and Trent were practically engaged. He had nothing against the young man, but he was a keen observer of human nature, and from what he'd observed of Faith when she and Trent were together…well, he just wasn't convinced she felt about him the same way he seemed to feel about her. That observation had made him even happier that Faith had decided to move with them to Wentworth Cove. A little distance might be just what their relationship needed. If it survived almost two thousand miles, that was one thing. But he wasn't counting on it.

"We could always invite him over for one of my world-famous barbecues. Tell him we want to thank him for helping Daniel…which is not untrue. It might give you a greater level of trust once you get to know the young man. If he's available Saturday, I can polish up my sermon Friday and have Saturday open."

"That's a good idea. Why don't you call him? That way you can tell him what will be on the menu and see if he's a vegetarian or a vegan or something. I don't know about these people up here. For some reason I don't think they eat a lot of barbecue."

Andy had to chuckle at his wife. She really was a Texas girl, and it was going to take her some time to warm up to this new home. He hoped she could, though, because he really liked the church, the congregation, and the town and thought he could stay here for a very long time…but only if his family was happy, too.

"I'll do that, Em. Leave it to me. And I don't disagree with you about needing to know more about someone who's spending time with our son. I might be a little too trusting of people. I'm glad I have you to rein me in and remind me that there really is such a thing as 'stranger danger'…like we used to tell the kids when they were younger."

"How do you like your steak? I can do rare, medium or well done," Daniel asked Josh as he entered the Parkers' backyard the next Saturday.

"Can you make mine medium? A little pink in the middle?" Josh replied.

"Sure. That's how I like mine. And how Dad likes his. Mom and Faith want theirs well done. That's girls for you."

Josh laughed. "I'm impressed. So you're both a photographer and a chef?"

"Daniel is my junior grill-master-in-training. I'm going to turn this operation over to him completely in another year or two." Andy shook Josh's hand. "We're glad you could make it. We wanted to do something to thank you for the photography lessons."

"We've had only one photo session so far, but we'll plan more soon. Did you learn anything from the last one, Daniel?"

"Well. Um. The thing I remember most is that sunsets look better when there are some clouds. Oh yeah. And to always turn around and look behind me when I'm taking a picture of a sunset. The sky was *pink*, Dad!"

"Yeah? Sounds like you had a very profitable session already. What do you have in mind for the next one, Josh? If you've even had time to give it some thought."

"I was wondering if you'd like to go into Portland and shoot some of the buildings downtown and boats in the harbor, Daniel. That is, if it's all right with you, Mr. Parker. And, of course, your sister is welcome to come with us, too. I know a great pizza place you both might like."

"Pizza! Sure! When can we go? Is it okay, Dad?"

"Josh, call me Andy. 'Mr. Parker' makes me feel old…and that's coming soon enough on its own. I don't see why not, son. Why don't you let me watch the grill for a while and run in the house and ask Faith. When did you have in mind, Josh?"

"What about next Saturday? I have a busy week in front of me, but I'm free on Saturday."

"Cool. BRB. That's 'be right back,' Dad." And with that, Daniel darted into the house.

"That boy is either keeping me young or making me old. I'm not sure which," Andy said.

"He seems like a good kid."

"He is. He's just full of energy. Much more outgoing than his sister…as you've probably noticed. She opens up once she gets to know you. But he opens up in order to get to know you."

"Dad!" Daniel opened the back door and hollered. "Mom wants to know how much longer for the steaks. Everything else is ready."

"They're probably ready now. I'll check. Bring me a sharp knife and a platter."

"Okay. I'll tell her."

"I'll say grace," Andy said, as the Parkers began to bow their heads. Josh was unaccustomed to grace before meals but followed suit, furtively glancing across the table at Faith before looking down at his plate. "Our Father in Heaven, we're thankful for this food, the ones who prepared it, and our new friend, Josh. Bless the food to nourish our bodies so that we can serve you better. Amen."

"Pass the mashed potatoes, please," Daniel said almost before the *Amen* was out.

"Hold on, son. Everything will get around to you. We're going to serve our guest first. Josh, why don't you start the potatoes and then pass them to Daniel."

"Sure. Everything looks and smells really good, Mrs. Parker. I don't get many home-cooked meals in Portland. In fact, I eat out at least ninety percent of the time."

"We're glad you could join us. Cooking is a family affair for the Parkers most of the time. Andy and Daniel take care of the meat, mainly on the grill, and Faith and I do the salads and vegetables. We don't usually have dessert, but this is a special occasion, so there's a surprise in the kitchen."

"I saw it, so I'm gonna eat fast. You'll like it, Josh. It's Faith's specialty," Daniel announced.

"Slow down, son. It's not going anywhere. We're not going to have dessert until everyone finishes."

"A Southern dish, I presume?" Josh asked, eyeing a blushing Faith across the table.

"I guess you could call—"

"It's pecan pie, and we brought the pecans with us from Texas!" Daniel exclaimed, unable to contain his excitement.

"Well, it's no longer a surprise, but Faith does make a great pecan pie. We missed these the four years she was away at college. I think you'll like it, Josh. But if you don't, I'm sure Daniel will be happy to help you out." Andy, an obviously proud dad, smiled at Faith.

Josh was as unaccustomed to loving family chatter at dinner as he was to grace before meals. On the rare occasions his family sat down together for a meal, they ate in relative silence or talked about who was suing whom or who would make partner next in their law practice. Compliments were rarely, if ever, handed out.

"I'm sure I will." Josh said, looking again at Faith, who was smiling at her dad.

"Tell us about your family, Josh." Emily made her move. She'd waited as long as she could to find out more about this young man who was spending time with her children. This young man about whom she knew absolutely nothing except that for some reason he'd changed his mind about giving Daniel some tips on photography. And her mother's intuition told her it might have more to do with her daughter than it did with her son.

"My parents are both attorneys in Boston. I grew up there. There's not much to tell really. I'm glad to be in Portland. It's a great city. Not as big. Not as congested."

"Do you have any brothers or sisters?"

An uncomfortable silence of a few seconds ensued before Josh responded. "Um. No. I don't."

Faith, as if sensing his unease, spoke up. "Josh, would you help me bring the pie and pie plates into the dining room."

"Of course." He said, following her to the kitchen.

"You were rescuing me, weren't you?" Josh said when they were out of hearing range of the others. "You didn't really need help with the plates. Am I right?"

"Maybe."

"Thanks."

"Sure. My mom likes to know everything about everybody. She doesn't mean anything by it. It's just her way of getting to know people. She wants all the information up front so she can relax and draw you into the fold." Faith uncovered the pie and got the dessert plates out of the china hutch and the forks out of the drawer.

"I'm sorry I hesitated. It's just that—" Josh hesitated again. *It's just that what? It's just that if I don't talk about it to people I've known for a long time, I'm not going to talk about it to people I just met...no matter how nice they are.*

"You don't have to explain anything. You have a right to your privacy. I'm a pretty private person myself. Here. Can you take these plates and forks? I'll cut and serve the pie at the table. I'm sure Daniel doesn't want to wait any longer."

"He's a good kid."

"The best. I love him so much."

"And he's lucky to have a sister like you."

"Hey, Faith," Daniel blurted when she and Josh returned to the dining room. "I forgot to ask you. Josh wants to take us to shoot some buildings and boats…uh, I forget where. Josh? Where was it we were going to take pictures and eat pizza?"

"Portland. It's about thirty minutes from here. It's not as big as Dallas, but I think you'll like it."

"Pizza, huh?" Faith knew food was one way to her little brother's heart, and Josh had caught on quickly. Evidently, the magic Daniel worked on people was working on Josh now. He seemed to be warming up to this boy he had no interest in earlier.

"Yeah. Next Saturday. Want to go?" Daniel had a hard time maintaining his cool when pizza was on the line.

"Well, I'll have to consult my schedule," Faith said, looking at her phone for a second and grinning. "No. I don't think I have any pressing appointments for next Saturday. And how could I turn down pizza in Portland? Sure, buddy. Let's do it."

"Good. It's a date then." Josh smiled. If this was the only way to see Faith, for a while anyway, he would take it.

Chapter Seven

Summer in Wentworth Cove continued to be so much like spring in Texas that Faith couldn't believe school would be starting in only a couple of weeks. Where was the heat? The drought? In their place were mild days, cool nights, and lots of midday showers. Just the kind of weather conducive to the flowers that made New England beautiful in the summer. Faith especially loved the window boxes overflowing with trailing geraniums, petunias, and periwinkles.

Josh had continued to give Daniel pointers about his camera and take him and Faith to places around the Portland and Kennebunk areas to take pictures. Faith suspected Josh was even growing quite fond of Daniel. When he told them that fall was just around the corner, she couldn't help but wonder where summer had gone. The temperature had broken ninety only a couple of days. Were there only three seasons here?

"Where are we going today?" Daniel asked, jumping into the backseat of Josh's Jeep on a mild, sunny afternoon in August.

"Have you ever seen a lighthouse?" Josh couldn't wait to show them Portland Head Light on Cape Elizabeth, just forty-five minutes north of Wentworth Cove. Sitting precipitously on a promontory like a king protecting his domain, its majesty was beyond compare, especially when the waves of the Atlantic furiously crashed against the rugged rocks below. If you stood in just the right place, you could feel the spray on your face and taste the salt of the ocean on your tongue.

Faith had continued to accompany Josh and Daniel on their photo-taking expeditions, partly because Daniel was always happy to have her along, partly because Emily could relax more knowing Daniel wasn't alone with Josh, who was still a relatively unknown entity, but mostly because she enjoyed the outings every bit as much as Daniel did.

She had met only one other person her age since moving, and Faith didn't think she and Annie Culwell had much in common. They had, however, met for lunch a couple of times since Annie seemed eager to get to know the new family in town. Faith told Annie about Trent, and Annie told Faith about a guy she'd met in Kennebunkport and had gone out with a couple of times. She offered to set Faith up with his friend, but Faith declined, saying she still hadn't decided to date anyone but Trent. It wasn't exactly a lie, but she wasn't sure what she'd say to Josh if he asked her out. She had thought he might a couple of times, but it hadn't happened.

She was pretty sure Trent hadn't dated anyone else, and she was feeling a little guilty for her thoughts about Josh...even though she and Trent had agreed to date other people if they wanted.

"Faith, have we ever seen a lighthouse? Do they have them in Texas? What is a lighthouse, anyway?" Daniel asked.

"No, I don't think you've ever seen one...and I've seen them only in pictures. Is that where we're going today?"

Faith had come to expect surprises from Josh. He enjoyed springing new places on them each time they met for a photo session. They'd been to Portland, Kennebunkport, and Goose Rocks Beach, but he was especially excited to show them Portland Head Light.

"Yep. It's a fun place to photograph, especially at sunset and on a windy day like today when the waves are high. I think you'll enjoy watching them crash against the rocks. Daniel, I want you to take it from several different angles and at several different times, and today we're going to talk about how the light is going to change soon."

"You mean when the sun goes down?"

"Well, that. Also, when the seasons change, the sun comes from a different direction and that affects the shadows and everything else about your photography. Fall's almost here, and you haven't seen anything until you've seen a New England autumn."

"I'm pretty sure I blinked and missed summer." While Faith marveled at the coolness of New England, Trent had been reporting on the sweltering heat in Dallas.

"No. This *is* summer. Do you like it?"

"It's nice, yeah."

"Maybe you'll like summer well enough to stay past our frigid winter and enjoy another one or two or three summers." A guy could hope, couldn't he? Remembering why he was here, ostensibly anyway, Josh turned to his young protégée. "Daniel, when the weather starts turning cooler, the sun moves gradually from the north to the south...so instead of setting in the northwest, it sets in the southwest. You'll notice that the shadows it casts are different. Then you have to learn to position your camera a little differently to capture the light the way you want it to appear in your photographs."

"That sounds complicated."

"It's not. You'll see. I'll walk you through it when the time comes."

Faith strolled around Portland Head Light, observing it from first one direction and then another. She thought it was one of the most majestic structures she'd ever seen, and learning that it was the oldest lighthouse in Maine made it all the more interesting to her.

"I appreciate what you're doing for Daniel," she told Josh when she saw him packing up his camera equipment. "My parents do, too. It's helped him survive summer in a new place where he hasn't met anyone his age yet. He lives for these outings with you. So thanks."

"I've enjoyed them, too. He's a cool kid. And a fast learner. He's taken some really great shots, don't you think? We'll get into editing and printing soon, but I wanted to work with him in the field first. I'm not packing up to go home. I'm going to shadow him for a while and see what he can do on his own. I think he's having fun."

"Oh, he is. And thanks for not minding me tagging along. It's helped me fill the hours waiting for school to start, too."

"You're a kindergarten teacher, right?"

"My first year. Yeah. I graduated in May, and the next week my parents told me they were moving to Maine...of all places. I'd heard of Maine, of course, but it always seemed many lifetimes away from Texas."

"Is it?"

"What?"

"Is it as foreign as you thought it would be?"

"It's pretty different, but I'm glad I came. It's not different in a bad way. I'm loving this weather...and the beauty of the area...especially the ocean. Loved it when we went to Goose Rocks Beach a couple of weeks ago."

"What about Portland Head Light?"

"It's so beautiful in a whole different way. So stately. So photogenic. A perfect place to bring Daniel. Speaking of—"

"Yeah. I see him over there. He's snapping away. I think I'll take him to my apartment next week and begin to show him how to use my editing equipment. It's pretty much a bachelor pad, but you're welcome to come, too. I'm pretty sure your mom still isn't comfortable with letting him go somewhere alone with me. Am I right?"

"She has no reason not to trust you, but she might be a little overly protective. Dad's tried to get her to lighten up, but so far he hasn't had much luck. Daniel doesn't talk about it, but he had leukemia when he was three. I think Mom feels like he's skating on thin ice and if he makes a wrong move, he'll fall through. He's been in remission for six years now, but there's always, in the back of her mind, the thought that it will return. Or maybe that something else will happen to him. I don't know…I'm talking too much, aren't I?"

"No. Not at all. I like to hear you talk. May you never, even if you live here the rest of your life, lose that accent."

Faith didn't know why, but every time Josh said something about her, she could feel her face flush. Could feel the redness rushing up her chest and her neck and onto her face. She'd never felt that with Trent and wondered whether it meant she was more comfortable with him or that Josh affected her in a way Trent never had.

Chapter Eight

Faith straightened her navy pencil skirt and looked down at her shoes, wondering why she'd chosen such high heels on the first day of school. She stood at the door of her kindergarten class like a sentinel, ready to welcome her new charges. She'd prepared her whole life for this, so why were her knees shaking? Why were her palms sweaty? She wanted everything to be perfect for her students. Knew this day would be so important for both them and their parents. Faith had excelled at student teaching, but in the back of her mind, she'd known then she could always defer to her supervising teacher if something went wrong or if she had a question. Now she was on her own and wanted to prove herself worthy of the confidence her new principal, Carrie Randolph, and the kindergarten team captain, Marilyn Hawkins, had placed in her when they hired her.

"Are you ready for this?" Hannah Sharpe called to her from across the hall.

"I think so, but I'll admit to some first-day jitters. Did you have them when you started?"

"Are you kidding? I get them every year. I have them right now. I don't know if it's nerves or just excitement. You'll feel like a pro by the time lunch rolls around, and then you'll get to start over with a new class in the afternoon. That's when you can correct any mistakes you think you might have made in the morning. My afternoon class always benefits because I get to practice on my morning class."

Faith was the only new kindergarten teacher at Kennebunk Elementary School, and Hannah was the only other teacher she'd met who was close to her age. Faith suspected she was twenty-five or younger. All the other teachers at this kindergarten-through-third-grade school appeared to be the age of her mother…or her grandmother. She guessed there wasn't much teacher turnover here and wondered how she'd be accepted. Would they think her too young for the task…or would they welcome fresh blood and new ideas? Time would tell, but today she was focused on her students, on making them feel good about being in school and want to come back tomorrow.

Faith heard voices in the next hall and Hannah said, "Sounds like kindergarten orientation is over. Here they come. Break out the tissues. See you at lunch."

"Hey. You're new here, aren't you?" Daniel turned to see a boy, a couple of inches taller than he was, walking toward him with two others in tow.

"Yeah. I'm Daniel. Just moved here this summer from Texas."

"Texas! Hey, guys. This here dude's from Texas. Where are your boots? Where's your cowboy hat? Did you ride your horse to school?" The three boys snickered, but Daniel wasn't sure what was so funny.

"I don't have a horse. I have some boots, but I don't wear them to school."

"You're from Texas, and you don't have a horse? What kind of Texan are you anyway?"

"You mean you've never been there?" Daniel shot back. "We actually ride in cars in Texas. You should see the skyscrapers in Dallas. Have you ever seen a building that's seventy-two stories tall? I guess you think Texas still looks like some of those old cowboy movies your grandpa watches. Well, it doesn't. It looks a lot newer than Maine."

"Hey! Don't get mad. We're just kidding. I'm Landon, and this is Michael, and this is Dylan," he said pointing to the other two.

"Hey," they each said.

Landon, obviously the leader of the pack, asked, "What class do you have first? Let me see your schedule."

Daniel unwrapped a neatly folded piece of paper and handed it to Landon.

"You have science with Mr. Hatfield. So do I. My brother had him a couple of years ago. Says he's pretty cool. Want me to show you where the room is?"

"Sure," Daniel said, thinking maybe this Landon wouldn't be such a problem after all.

"Bye, guys," Landon called back to Michael and Dylan as he and Daniel walked away. "Me and Tex'll catch up with you at lunch."

Daniel had been wondering all summer if he would have to eat lunch by himself the first day...and maybe even the first week...of school. It seemed now as though his worries were over. Landon might have some weird opinions about Texas, but at least Daniel was relieved he wouldn't have to eat alone.

"Hey, bud. How was your first day? How many new friends do you have? Bet you can't count them on one hand." Faith's school was only a few blocks from Daniel's so she would be driving him and picking him up each day that she didn't have to stay late for a staff meeting.

"It was okay. I met a cool guy. He has some crazy ideas about Texas, but he's pretty nice. His name's Landon and we have two classes together, social studies and science. I met a couple of other guys, too, but they weren't very friendly."

"So all in all it was a pretty good day?"

"I guess . . ." he said, his voice trailing off. "I can't get my locker open, though."

"Did you tell anyone?"

"No. I've never had a locker before. I didn't know who to tell."

"I'll bet you could tell one of your teachers. Were your teachers nice?"

"Yeah. They were real nice. I don't think they know I just moved here. We didn't do much in my classes today. Just went over rules and supplies and stuff."

"It might be a good idea to tell one of them about your locker tomorrow. You might need a place to keep your books when you don't have homework. If someone at school can't help you, I'll come in when I pick you up tomorrow and see what I can do."

"Homework! I already have homework tonight! Can you believe it? The first day of school. I *knew* sixth grade was gonna be harder than fifth! Oh yeah. And there's no recess either, but I might join the basketball team. Landon's going to." Daniel realized he hadn't asked Faith about her first day. "Do you like your school?"

"Yeah, buddy, I do. My classes are small, and all the students were on their best behavior today. I think most of them were a little scared. Some cried when their parents left so I dried a few tears, but for the most part, it was a really good first day of teaching. I'm sure I'll feel even better about it after I've been there a while. Just like you'll probably be ruling middle school in a few weeks. And I'm *sure* you'll rule the basketball court."

"Like a boss!"

"Daniel 'Like a Boss' Parker. That's the little brother I know and love."

Chapter Nine

"Hey, Josh! Guess what I learned in school this week? Do you know what a mentor is?" A few weeks into the school year, Josh was in Daniel's room at home, teaching Daniel how to upload his photos to an editing application on his laptop and giving him step-by-step instructions on cropping, color, and contrast.

"I think I do, but why don't you tell me."

"There was this guy named Mentor who was an adviser to Tel...Telem...oh, I forget his name. Anyway he was Odysseus's son."

"Telemachus?"

"Yeah. How'd you know?"

"*The Odyssey* was one of my favorite things I read in high school. For some reason I remember almost everything about it."

"Well anyway, we learned about him today and my teacher told us what a mentor is, and I was thinking you're my mentor in photography."

"I guess I am. Yeah. And you're a really fast learner. How're those new uploads coming along? Have you finished cropping them? Ready for me to take a look?"

"Daniel, dinner's ready," Emily called from downstairs. "Josh, will you stay and eat with us? There's plenty."

"No, thanks, I'd bet—"

"Yeah, stay! Please!" Daniel begged.

"Well, I really need to get back to Portland...but...I guess—"

"He'll stay, Mom," Daniel shouted back down the stairs.

"Your mom's going to think she's adopted me if I keep eating with you guys every time I come over." Josh was growing quite fond of the Parker family...not only Faith and Daniel, but Andy and Emily, too. They were so different from his parents, so laid-back and down-to-earth. Meals were casual and happy. The Parkers talked about what they had done during the day, each one catching up with the others. And the funny part about it was that they all seemed interested in each other. They sat at a round table, so pulling up one or two more chairs didn't seem to be a problem. And Emily always cooked way too much food for just four people. It was as if she always prepared for dinner guests.

A couple of weeks earlier she'd told Josh to call her Emily instead of Mrs. Parker. He felt she was trusting him more with Daniel, but he wondered how she'd feel if she knew how he felt about Faith. The more time he spent around her, the more he admired her, the more he wanted to be alone with her, to talk to her—just the two of them—wanted to get to know the real Faith Parker. Wanted to touch her shiny auburn hair, breathe in her perfume, kiss the sprinkling of freckles that danced across her face.

He'd thought about asking her out on a real date, but he didn't want Daniel to think he was using him to get close to his sister. If he was honest, he'd have to admit that's how it was at first, but he'd grown to like Daniel for Daniel's sake, and now Faith was in a totally separate category. He'd also held off on asking her out because of Trent. Daniel had filled him in on their relationship, and not knowing how serious they were, he was in a quandary. Should he take a risk…or wait it out? He had no idea if he had even the slightest chance of gaining her affections.

"This meal is great as usual, Emily," Josh said as Andy passed him the Brussels sprouts for the second time. "I've never eaten Brussels sprouts that tasted this good. In fact, I never used to eat them at all."

"I was blessed to get a wife who's not only sweet and beautiful but a world-class cook, too, wasn't I, Josh?" Andy smiled at his wife, and Josh couldn't remember ever hearing his dad say anything like that about his mother. Maybe if they'd discussed something besides trials and codicils at dinnertime…

"Daniel, did you have a snack after school?" Emily asked her son.

"No. Why?"

"You haven't eaten much tonight. Do you feel okay?"

"I was thinking the same thing, Em. Something wrong, son? You've been kind of quiet tonight, too. How about some more mashed potatoes to finish off that meatloaf?" Andy picked up the bowl and handed it across the table toward Daniel.

"I don't want any, Dad. I'm just tired. Maybe it's basketball practice. I have to work really hard to keep up with Landon."

"You don't have to keep up with Landon, son. You just have to keep up with *you*. Do *your* best. That's all Mom and I will ever ask of you. And I'll bet that's all your coach asks of you, too."

"Me, too, bud," Faith said. "You know we're proud of you whether you play basketball or not."

"Well, I guess that makes it unanimous," Josh chimed in. "You're a first-class photographer, and you don't have to compete with anyone on that."

"That's cool, y'all, but I really want to be a good basketball player. I like it. I guess I can tell Coach Miller when I'm feeling tired. I felt like I was gonna throw up this afternoon, but I kept playing. Guess I shouldn't have."

Andy took another scoop of potatoes for himself. "Next time you feel that way, tell Coach. I'll bet he'll let you sit out for a few minutes and catch your breath. He wouldn't have much of a team if his players start getting sick, now would he?"

"I guess not. Can I be excused? I need to finish cropping the pics I uploaded so Josh can look at them before he goes home. Will you, Josh?"

"Sure. Just let me finish up here. I don't want your mom to get the idea I don't like her cooking."

"You *may* be excused, Daniel. And Josh," Emily said, "I can tell you like my cooking, and it makes me happy to be able to pay you back in a small way for spending so much time with Daniel. It's really helped him adjust to living in a new place where he didn't have any friends."

"Hey, he's a cool kid. Hard not to like. I think I'll go up and see how he's coming with the crops before I head back to Portland. Thanks for another great meal."

"Hannah, I need to ask you something. Will you tell me if I'm just being paranoid?" Hannah Sharpe had become Faith's go-to person at Kennebunk Elementary. A couple of times she'd asked Hannah about a discipline situation, and Hannah had been the voice of reason. *Or maybe the voice of experience*, Faith thought. *After all, she's taught for four years, so she's run into more of these situations than I have.*

Although Marilyn Hawkins was the kindergarten team leader and she should go to her first with a problem, Marilyn didn't exactly exude "warm and fuzzy." She wasn't the kind of kindergarten teacher Faith wanted to emulate or ask for advice. In fact, Faith was put off by her gruff manner. She'd heard through the grapevine that her students were, too. She couldn't imagine someone of Marilyn's disposition teaching a room full of five-year-olds. They needed nurturing...hugs and praise...not constant scolding and a totally regimented classroom. Faith's classroom might be a little noisier than Marilyn's at times, but that's when real learning took place. The children seemed to be enjoying themselves, too. Who said learning and fun couldn't take place simultaneously?

"Sure. Shoot," Hannah said, as she absentmindedly stirred a spoonful of sugar into her coffee. She and Faith had fallen into a routine of meeting in the teachers' lounge for coffee and debriefing each morning before their students showed up. "Hey, I don't mind talking about anything. You and I seem to share a teaching philosophy, and we might be the only two on the team who think the way we do. It's nice to finally have a comrade."

"Well, tell me if I should worry about this. Marilyn came into my room the other day on her break and my kids were working in groups. True, they were a little noisy, but I was circulating around the room, and they were all on task. They were just excited about what they were discovering about the ocean. One group was learning about plant life in the ocean, the second one was learning about animal life, and the third one was learning about what makes the ocean salty. Then they were going to rotate stations."

"How were they learning?"

"They were watching and listening to videos on iPads. After that, they were talking in their groups about what they'd learned and they were really excited about it. Yeah, it was a little noisy, but my student teaching supervisor said, 'There's nothing wrong with noise when real learning is happening.'"

"So what's the problem?"

"I'm pretty good at reading people, and I could tell she wasn't happy. She wants to talk to me after school today."

"Seriously, she's been teaching since dinosaurs roamed the earth. She has no concept of or appreciation for innovative teaching methods. She thinks the kids should be quiet all the time, and I think her students are afraid to say anything in her classroom. Coincidentally, they're usually the ones who get in trouble at recess. They have to let that energy out sometime… But I don't think you have anything to worry about. She's the team leader because she's been here the longest, but Carrie Randolph will back you. She's all about innovative teaching methods and knows that kids can have fun and learn at the same time. Frankly, I don't know why she lets Marilyn stay on as team leader, but that's the way it was when she came here as principal and she hasn't rocked the boat."

"That makes me feel better. Mrs. Randolph's been really nice to me. I think she likes me. I just don't want her to think she made a mistake in hiring me…especially because I haven't taught before."

"Don't worry about that. She took a chance on me, too, when no one else would. I will tell you this, though. She vets all the candidates well. She talked to everyone I'd ever come into contact with regarding education. My student teaching supervisor, my supervising teacher, a couple of my education professors. Even checked with all my personal references. She left no stone unturned, and I'm pretty sure she did the same with you. So by the time she's ready to make an offer, she knows you and your teaching philosophy and methods. Honestly, Faith, it won't come as a surprise to her that your students can learn without being as regimented as little soldiers."

"Okay. Good."

"Text me after your meeting with Marilyn, though. I'm curious as to how she can turn a positive learning situation into something negative. Other than that, what's going on? How do you like living here? I know you must miss your boyfriend in Texas."

"I do, but I've stayed busy and we FaceTime a lot. He's busy too…starting a new job and all. I don't think the move's been as hard on either one of us as we thought it would be."

"Yeah? Have you met someone else?"

"You mean a guy?"

"Yes. Well? That look on your face is kind of giving you away. Could that be the reason the move hasn't been overly difficult?"

"It's really nothing…"

"No, no, no. I know 'nothing' when I see it, and this is not 'nothing.' Tell all."

"Well…" Faith hesitated.

"C'mon. You owe me since I made you feel better about Marilyn. Talk."

"There's this guy who's working with my brother. He's a photographer, and I got Daniel a camera for Christmas. He's showing him how to focus, crop, edit…stuff like that."

"And?"

"And…"

"And I'm guessing he's hot?"

"Depends on what you call 'hot.' He's not like Trent at all. Doesn't look like him. Doesn't act like him. Not the kind of guy I thought I'd ever be interested in."

"But you are. Right?"

"I think I could be, but…"

"But? Help me out here. I'm having to drag this out of you."

"But he's just not the type I ever pictured myself with. Trent's got ambition. A good job. Totally conventional.

Likes to wear a suit to work. Kind of a neat freak, but I can live with that."

"So what's Mr. Hottie like?"

"Pretty much the opposite. Graduated from Harvard in pre-law."

"Doesn't sound opposite to me."

"He's a photographer."

"You mean that's his *job*? With a degree in pre-law from Harvard? I bet his parents aren't very happy about *that*."

"He hasn't really talked about it, but I get the feeling he's not close to his parents. And that's kind of a red flag for me. I guess it's because I am close to mine, but I always assumed any guy I dated would have the same kind of relationship with his parents that I have with mine."

"Maybe he has a reason. Maybe it's a *good* reason. Has he ever talked about it?"

"Not to me. He doesn't talk about his family at all. And something kind of strange happened a few weeks ago…the first time he ate dinner with us."

"What?"

"My mom… You'd have to know her to appreciate this. She wants to know everything about everybody. She asked him about his family. He said his mom and dad are attorneys."

"Uh oh. I smell trouble."

"Yeah. Well, then she asked him if he had any brothers or sisters, and he didn't say anything for a couple of seconds. It was like he had to think about it. Then he said no. But he seemed uneasy about the whole situation."

"Oooh. I love a good mystery. You'll have to figure this out and fill me in."

"I'm not going to ask him again. If he wants me to know, it will be because he decided to tell me."

"How often do you see him? And have you two ever been alone together?"

"Not *really* alone, no."

"Ask him out."

"I can't do that."

"Why not? Because of Trent?"

"No. Trent and I have an understanding. We're not tied down. He wanted to be, but I don't think that would make for a healthy relationship."

"What's the problem then?"

"That's just not my style. Maybe I'm a little old-fashioned, but I think they guy should make the first move."

"I hope Mr. Hottie is old-fashioned, too. Does he know about Trent?"

"He does. Daniel's talked about him a little."

"That's the problem. He's not going to make a move if he thinks you're spoken for."

"Maybe he doesn't *want* to 'make a move.'"

"Are you kidding? You're smart, pretty, great with kids. You cook, too, don't you?"

"A little. Nothing like my mom."

"See. A guy would have to be crazy not to want to date you."

"Thanks, Hannah, but I don't know. He probably doesn't think I'm *his* type."

"Well, I'm just saying. Maybe you should at least drop a few hints."

At the sound of the bell, Faith and Hannah headed for their rooms, bending down to accept hugs from kindergartners along the way. "This conversation isn't over," Hannah called from across the hall when they were both standing outside their rooms as their students rushed in. "You might have to make the first move this time, for obvious reasons. Oh, let me know how your meeting goes, too."

Chapter Ten

If Andy Parker were completely honest, he'd have to admit his weekly trips to the Kennebunk Public Library were as much to talk to John Strong, Kennebunk's revered head librarian, as to use the library's reference room to prepare his Sunday sermon. John fascinated Andy with his fatherly countenance and wisdom, and the younger man looked forward to these visits even more than using the library's reference books.

Yellow, orange, red, and maroon leaves glimmered in the breeze as he made his way along Summer Street to the library. What was it Josh had told Daniel about how the light would change in the fall? "As the sun moves to the south, it casts a different type of light on everything. The trees are lighted from a different angle, and there's a slight change in the way shadows fall," he said. "A photographer needs to know these things."

Andy thought this was the most beautiful fall he'd ever seen. Was it because his eyes were more open now to the changing light, the changing colors, than they'd been before? Was it because he was looking specifically for changes in the way shadows moved ever so gradually from one side of an object to the other as summer morphed into fall? Was it because he was both happy and at complete peace with his and Emily's decision to make the move from their native state of Texas to the uncharted waters of Wentworth Cove, Maine? And it didn't hurt that Faith had come with them. He would have hated to be so far away from his daughter as she began her career.

"Andy, it's always good to see a Texas expat here in our little library." John greeted him as soon as he entered the large double doors.

"It's good to be a Texas expat this time of year, but I'm not sure I'll feel that way come December and January. I've been warned."

"You learn to dress for it," John assured him. "What can I do for you this fine fall day?"

"Do you have a minute?"

"Sure. Come into my office. I was just about to have a cup of tea. How about it? Or coffee?"

"Tea sounds good if it's not too much trouble."

"Tea it is. What's on your mind, Reverend?"

"Nothing earth-shattering. I was just wanting to get a little more history of the area and some of the people who live here, and I thought it would be more interesting coming from you than from a book. I don't even know if such a book exists."

"Actually I put together a short book on Kennebunk, Kennebunkport, and Wentworth Cove about thirty years ago, but there have been a lot of changes since then, especially since George Bush made Walker's Point and Ocean Avenue tourist attractions."

"I guess I'm more interested in the people who live in the area now…and their history. For instance, the Weilers. I know Miriam is the mayor and her husband Isaac is editor of the weekly paper. The Herringtons. I've heard their ancestors were the first inhabitants of Wentworth Cove. Are there other notable citizens? I just like to know as much about my town as possible. It not only helps in sermon preparation, but also Em and I like to become involved in the whole community."

"You know Kate Norsworthy. Her family has lived in Wentworth Cove as long as mine. We both grew up there. She lost her husband about ten years ago in a small private plane crash. So tragic. They were totally devoted to one another and their two sons, David and Nathan."

"We know Kate. She was the first to welcome us when we moved in. I've met her family, too…David, Elizabeth, Jessica, Nathan, Tracy. And doesn't Tracy's mother visit Wentworth Cove often…Laura, I think?" Andy was amazed and pleased at how easily he'd been able to insert Laura into the conversation.

"She does. You've probably seen us together."

"Now that you mention it…" Andy smiled at the older man.

"There's quite a story there. How much time do you have? And are you in the least interested?"

"All afternoon and definitely."

"True confession time then," John started. "I met Tracy's mother, Laura, the summer before Tracy was born. She was spending a couple of months in Wentworth Cove while her husband studied abroad. At Oxford, I think. We became friends. Actually, for me it was more than a friendship. I fell in love with her before I realized she was married. When she casually mentioned her husband, it was too late. I was totally smitten. She, of course, saw me as just a friend. We had so much in common as we're both librarians. Talked about writers and books and libraries for hours on end.

"You're probably wondering why I didn't see a ring and realize I was falling in love with a married woman, but her ring was an opal rather than a diamond, so I just assumed… By the time she mentioned her husband, there was no turning back for me. For my heart anyway. For the way I felt about her. Of course, I would never... Well, you know I..."

"John, this is a fascinating story and I'm not making any judgments here."

"I guess you're also wondering how we got back together after so many years."

"I'll have to admit you've piqued my curiosity."

"Last summer Tracy came to our village for a month-long vacation. She found out about our friendship that summer and because her birth was nine months after that summer, well you can imagine what she might have thought. But her father had come back to the States for a long weekend, so when she found out about that, she and I became friends and she brought her mother here for a weekend. My heart was pounding when she stepped off that plane. I guess I should also explain that Tracy's dad passed away about ten years ago. Tracy and he had been very close. I'm so glad that she has accepted me, not as a substitute dad, but as a friend. I think it would make her happy if Laura and I were to get married some day. I know it would make me incredibly happy."

"Would you think me too nosy, John, if I asked what the status of the relationship is now? I've seen you sitting together in church. She's a lovely lady. Her daughter looks a lot like her, don't you think?"

"Yes, I do. I think they're both beautiful. The status? I guess you'd say we're kind of at a standstill. We've been keeping company since that weekend Tracy brought her here last summer. She spends many weekends in Wentworth Cove. I've spent some weekends in Boston. And, yes, we've talked about getting married. I just don't think she's ready. So...I figure I've waited this long... I can be a very patient man, Andy."

"She's a fortunate lady. I wish you both the best. Guess I'd better do a little work now. Thanks for the tea...and the chat."

As Andy was thinking about his sermon for Sunday, he pondered what John had told him about Laura and his enduring love for her. "Love is patient and kind...hopes all things, endures all things" came to mind, and his sermon preparation took a whole different direction from what he had originally planned. He would talk to his congregation Sunday about love...about what it *really* was...not what so many people today *thought* it was. He put his head down and scribbled furiously as the words began to flow.

Chapter Eleven

The phone rang as Emily was polishing the imposing baby grand piano that held a place of prominence in the Parkers' living room. She hadn't played it much lately but resolved to change that as she admired the patina of the wood on the heirloom she'd brought into the marriage.

"Parker residence. This is Emily," she said, closing the fallboard to protect the keys.

"Mrs. Parker? This is Dwayne Miller. I'm Daniel's basketball coach."

Emily had lived for six years expecting to get a call or visit from someone telling her Daniel's leukemia had returned. Every time a teacher or a friend's parent called, her heart caught in her throat. "Is Daniel okay?"

"I think so, but he looked exhausted about halfway through practice, so I told him to go shower and get dressed. He's been getting tired a lot lately. I went in to check on him as he was getting dressed, and I saw some bruises on his upper leg. Do you know if he's fallen or run into anything lately?"

"Not that I know of." At the mention of bruises, Emily's heart skipped a beat. "Did you ask him about it?"

"I did, but he said he didn't know where they came from. Usually when we see something like this we have to notify Child Protective Services, but I wanted to talk with you and Reverend Parker first."

"Thank you so much. I'll call Andy as soon as we hang up. Should we make an appointment to come to your office...or would you like to come to our home? What do you think could be causing it? He's not the type to get into fights at school. Or have you observed otherwise?" What kind of mother would hope her son had gotten into a fight at school? But that's what Emily Parker was thinking. Better that than the alternative, for she knew the signs of leukemia and bruising was one of them. Fatigue and loss of appetite were two others. This was the news she'd been dreading. She was sure of it.

"Absolutely not. In fact, he's been a calming influence on the whole team. He's very well liked. They've nicknamed him Tex, you know."

"So he told us. He likes it. I think it makes him feel special."

"He's not our most talented player but quite a hustler on the court. Could you and your husband come to my office this evening...around seven or seven-thirty?"

"I'll call Andy now and have him call you, but I'm sure we can work that out. Thank you so much for letting us know about this." Emily quickly dialed Andy's number and immediately burst into tears.

"Hey, Em. How's your afternoon going? I should be home in about an hour. What's for dinner? I'm starving. Went to see John Strong today and completely forgot to eat lunch... Em? Are you crying?"

"Andy..." Emily said, tears choking her voice back.

"What's wrong, babe? You okay? The kids?"

"Coach Miller called."

"Yeah? Did Daniel get hurt in practice?"

As Emily relayed the basketball coach's concerns to her husband, he listened quietly. Andy knew what his wife was thinking, and he couldn't say it hadn't crossed his mind in the past couple of weeks, too…especially when Daniel left food on his plate and chose to lie down rather than ride his bicycle. Since their move, he and Faith had been exploring the area, riding up and down the picturesque back streets and paths of both Wentworth Cove and Kennebunkport. Lately, Daniel hadn't felt like riding his bike, saying he was too tired from basketball practice. Faith seemed to buy that explanation, but Andy had been concerned.

Combine that with bruises, and he was more than a little concerned. "I'll be right there. Don't say anything to the kids. Don't want to concern them unnecessarily."

"Oh, Andy!" Emily cried. "You know what I'm thinking."

"I know. I know. I'll be there soon."

"Faith, Dad and I are going to visit someone in the community after dinner. Will you be here?" Emily called after she'd dried her eyes and washed her face. Just knowing that Andy would be home soon had strengthened her. He was her rock, had been since they'd met in high school…and especially for the two years Daniel had undergone chemotherapy. Emily wouldn't leave her son's side and Andy had held the family together. He'd done the laundry, cooked the meals, dried the tears, picked up Faith from school every day. And all of this while continuing to pastor the church in Dallas.

Other friends had pitched in, too, running errands, preparing food, driving Faith to piano lessons and soccer practice. But Emily relied on Andy for emotional support, and he never let her down. She couldn't wait for him to get home.

"Sure, Mom. I'll be working on next week's lesson plans," Faith answered.

"I think Josh is coming by for a few minutes to help Daniel with his math. We really need to start paying that boy for all the photography and math tutoring he's done, but he won't hear of it. Says a meal every now and then is payment enough. I think he likes to be here during family time."

"He does seem to think up reasons to come over. Do you remember that at first he said he wouldn't meet with Daniel? I wonder what made him change his mind."

"Honey, I have a theory about that," Emily said with an air of mystery.

"What are you thinking?"

"Okay. But remember you asked. When we were at the Norsworthy Art Gallery for his one-man photography show… Do you remember that evening?"

"Sure."

"I saw you and Josh talking…just the two of you."

"Yeah?"

"And it was the Monday after the show that Jessica Norsworthy called to tell me he'd changed his mind. Interesting timing, don't you think?"

"Mom! You don't think…? No."

"Whatever you want to think, but moms know these things."

"You mean you think he's helping Daniel because of me? No. He hasn't given me any indication that's the case. I think he really likes Daniel."

"Of course he does. Who doesn't? I'm just saying he might have had another reason at first…and then when he got to know Daniel… I think he might have two reasons to come over now."

Faith peered out the window of her upstairs bedroom, pondering this revelation from her mother—halfway wishing it to be true—and watched as a light rain watered the rose garden below. How could it be raining while the sun was shining at the same time? The weather mirrored her feelings. There was something hidden and mysterious…and almost brooding…about him. That should have caused her to her keep her distance. But why did she get butterflies whenever she was in his presence? Why did she anticipate their time together…even when her little brother was going to be there, too?

Her thoughts centered on him more often than she felt comfortable admitting to herself. In school she'd find herself thinking about his mop of blond hair and how he'd shake his head to put it back in place when it appeared windblown. His grin that somehow made it seem as though even his light blue eyes were smiling. It was an image she couldn't seem to shake. An image that kept popping back into her consciousness. And now her mother had surmised that Josh was thinking about her, too. Why couldn't Daniel's photography mentor have been ugly? Why did he have to throw her off-kilter every time he talked to her? And how could she get her mind back on stable, reliable Trent?

She didn't know what to think about her mother's suspicions. Did Josh have an interest in her? Would she care if he did? How did she feel about him? What would all of this mean to her relationship with Trent? Maybe her decision to move hadn't been fair to him and their relationship. Maybe it hadn't been fair to her either. Maybe she should have stayed to give their relationship a chance to progress.

So far Daniel's presence when she and Josh were together had kept her feelings for Josh safe, but she wondered how they would act if they were alone for any length of time. Did he even want to be alone with her?

Was he holding back because of Trent? If that were the case, it would only elevate him in her eyes.

Maybe she should drop some hints as Hannah suggested. Faith's thoughts were interrupted by the doorbell. "I'll get it, Daniel," she called as she almost ran down the stairs. *Slow down. What has gotten into you? Have you forgotten you're FaceTiming with Trent later tonight?*

"Hi, Josh. My parents aren't here tonight. Daniel's waiting for you, though." *So was I, if you really want to know the truth.*

"That's okay. I don't want your mom to think I come over so often just to get a home-cooked meal," Josh grinned that crooked grin of his and Faith's knees grew weak.

"She's flattered that you like her cooking."

"Who wouldn't?"

"Well, Daniel's in his room. I'm going to work on some lesson plans. I'll see you later."

"Uh…Faith . . ." Josh hesitated.

"Yes?"

"I kind of wanted to talk to you first, if you have a minute."

"Sure."

"Well…" Josh stood there mute for what seemed to Faith like an unusual amount of time, considering he'd said he wanted to talk to her.

"Well?"

He shifted uneasily from one foot to the other.

"You're being pretty mysterious, you know," she prompted.

"Yeah. I'll get to the point." He cleared his throat nervously. "I know you have a boyfriend in Texas."

"Right?"

"Are you…you know…exclusive?"

"Exclusive?"

"Yeah. Excluding anyone else. Like if I wanted to ask you to go to dinner with me or something."

Faith's heart skipped a beat. She hadn't expected it this soon, yet here it was. "Are you asking me? To go to dinner with you?"

"Yes. Yes, I am."

"Oh, that's funny. I didn't hear a question in there anywhere," Faith teased.

"Faith Parker, will you go to dinner with me sometime…just us…without Daniel as a chaperon. If you want to, and if you don't think it will hurt his feelings not to be invited, and if it won't cause you a problem with the other guy."

"Trent. His name's Trent."

"With Trent…"

"That's a lot of *ifs*."

"One more. And *if* you'd like to dress up and go to Portland Harbor for lobster Saturday night."

"I…uh…"

"Look. I didn't mean to make you uncomfortable. I just thought—"

"No. I'd love to go. It's just that I haven't been out with anyone except Trent in over a year. But we have an understanding that we can date other people."

"We don't have to call it a date…if that would make you feel better."

"So you're *not* asking me on a date?"

"Well, I can be…or…" Josh nervously shifted his weight again. "Are you *always* this contrary?"

"Just ascertaining your intentions, sir."

"How's this? I intend to take you to Portland Harbor for the best lobster dinner you've ever had, and then I intend to take a stroll along the harbor and show you the lights of Portland. I intend to be with you and not Daniel this time. Don't get me wrong. I like Daniel. I mean I really like him, but I think he's chaperoned us long enough, and I'd like to be alone with you for an evening. So what do you think of those intentions, Miss Scarlet?"

"Why, Mistah Butlah, ah do believe you've made me blush."

"I don't think I heard a 'Yes, I'll be happy to go to Portland Harbor with you for an amazing lobster dinner Saturday night.' Don't leave me guessing here."

"Yes. I'd like to go."

"Great. I'm going up to talk to Daniel. I don't want him to feel left out. You know...I don't think I've ever asked a little brother for permission to date his sister before. Are we calling this a date?"

"Sounds like a date to me."

"Good. I'll talk to you again after I help him with math and pop the question."

Josh took the steps two at a time and waltzed into Daniel's room. "Hey, buddy. I hear you're having a little trouble with some word problems in math."

"I hate word problems."

"Here. Let me see what you're working on. We'll figure it out together," Josh assured him.

There was something about the way Josh explained things to Daniel. Something soft and patient and nurturing. Like the way he explained the camera. He made it so clear that Daniel had no problem understanding complex concepts that baffled him at school. Quickly and confidently he worked through the assigned problems using the method Josh showed him.

"Hey, Daniel. I need to get back to Portland, but I have something to ask you before I go," Josh announced when he could see he was no longer needed.

"Okay."

"I know you're crazy about your sister, right? She's pretty special to you, isn't she?"

"Yeah. She's my best friend." Daniel looked at Josh and his sensitive nature kicked in. "I don't mean to hurt your feelings. It's just that I've known her longer. But you're my best mentor."

"No problem. I'd expect you to like your sister more. The thing is…" Josh hesitated, not completely sure how to broach the subject.

"Yeah?"

"The thing is…" He decided on the direct approach. "I like her, too."

Daniel's eyes grew wide. "You mean, like, for a girlfriend?"

"Well, I mean I'd like to get to know her better. What would you think of that?"

"Cool!"

"I know she has a boyfriend in Texas. Do you think that would be a big problem?"

"Nah. I don't really like him that much anyway. He's okay, but he never talks to me much. I mean he never helped me with photography or math or anything like that like you do. So yeah! I think you should take my sister on a date!"

"That's a great idea. Do you think she'd go?"

"Go ask her right now."

"Now? Don't you want me to finish helping you with the math problems?"

"No. I got this…but come back up and tell me what she said."

"You got it. Be right back," Josh said, bounding out the door and heading for the stairs.

Waltzing into the kitchen where Faith was loading the dishwasher…and looking pleased with the way he'd handled the situation upstairs, he announced, "Daniel told me to come down and ask you for a date."

"He did, did he?"

"Didn't tell him we'd already gotten the formalities out of the way. This way he's happy because he thinks it was his idea."

One more thing to make him more likable, Faith thought. He was so considerate of her little brother. "That's really clever, Josh. He's crazy about you."

"I'm supposed to report back to him. Then I gotta head home. What if I pick you up at seven Saturday? I'll make reservations for seven-thirty."

"I'll be ready. Can't be late for lobster."

"Good. Be right back."

Josh was getting adept at taking the stairs in the Parkers' house two at a time. He rounded the corner into Daniel's room. "I'm taking your sister to dinner in Portland Saturday night. What do you think of that?"

"That's really cool."

"I'm glad you approve. That means a lot to me. Hey. Do you feel okay tonight?"

"I'm kind of tired. Must be this math homework. I hate homework."

"Well, take it easy. Call me if you need help with anything else. I'll see you Saturday night when I come to pick up Faith."

When Josh left, Daniel plopped down on his bed, still fully clothed but feeling as though if he closed his eyes, he would be asleep in no time. He remembered the two years of leukemia treatment, remembered losing his hair, remembered feeling sick and throwing up a lot. He didn't dwell on it, but sometimes he wondered if the cancer would come back. His parents took him for yearly checkups with Dr. Cameron, but now he wondered where he would go for a checkup when another year rolled around…or if he would have to go soon if he kept feeling like this.

His door was open and he could hear Faith talking to Trent in her room down the hall. "But what if I don't want to go along to get along? What if I think a method of teaching is important enough to fight for?" His sister rarely raised her voice, but it was louder than normal now. She'd told the family about her meeting with her supervisor, and he assumed that's what she was talking about to Trent. Apparently they were disagreeing about how she should handle the situation. Oh well. He didn't care. He was excited she'd agreed to go out with Josh. Josh would make a way cooler boyfriend for Faith anyway.

Chapter Twelve

The days were getting shorter, and it was almost dark when Emily and Andy arrived at Daniel's middle school and dialed Coach Miller's phone number. He'd said the school would be locked and he would have to let them in.

"Reverend and Mrs. Parker, thank you for coming. Have a seat." He motioned to a couple of metal folding chairs in front of his desk.

"It's Andy and Emily, and we want to thank you for meeting with us tonight, when I'm sure you'd rather be at home with your family," Andy said, pulling out a chair for his wife and then one for himself.

"My wife is used to this. She knew what she was signing up for when we married. She's a teacher, too, so no surprises when I have a late parent conference." Dwayne Miller had kind eyes that matched his dark chocolate-brown skin and a smile that made people feel as though he had all the time in the world for them.

Andy started. "We're concerned about the bruises you saw on Daniel. His legs, right? He hasn't worn shorts around the house since August, so we haven't noticed anything. And we didn't want to say anything to him until we talked with you."

"I'm sure you know, Andy, being a minister, that we're supposed to report anything we see like this to Child Protective Services."

"But—" Emily leaned slightly forward in her chair as if she anticipated having to go into mom-attack mode.

"We do. Of course," Andy interrupted his wife.

"But I wanted to talk with you first. I don't for a minute think this is a case of child abuse, but coupled with his recent lack of energy, I thought it was something that needed to be looked into. I suggest a complete physical."

"Of course that's what we'll do. As you know, we're new to the area. Is there someone you would recommend?"

"I don't know a pediatrician, but I have a great doctor in Portland. Let me give him a call and see what he thinks. I'll get back with you in a day or two. Meanwhile, if you want to ask around and find someone else, let me know."

"Thank you for your concern, Coach Miller. Daniel has enjoyed being on the team. It's helped him make the adjustment from Texas to Maine, which, as you can imagine, is a huge change for an eleven-year-old boy."

"As I told Emily this afternoon, we're happy to have him. He brings a lot to the team. I hope all is okay. I'll be in touch soon. Or you can call me anytime."

"Andy," Emily said as soon as they were in the car, "we have to call Dr. Cameron first thing in the morning."

"Why? He's in Dallas."

"He might know someone here who's a pediatric oncologist."

"Let's don't jump to conclusions, Em. Don't you want to schedule a thorough physical first before calling an oncologist?"

"Maybe," she halfway conceded, "but I'm putting together pieces of this puzzle, and I don't like what I'm coming up with. I don't know why we don't just skip the first step and see an oncologist. Otherwise, we might be wasting time."

"You're right. I think I'm in a little bit of denial. I'll call him as soon as his office opens in the morning. Meanwhile, there's nothing we can do but pray...and try to act normal. I don't think we should mention this to Faith yet. She has enough to think about with a new job and that supervisor she's dealing with."

"Come in, Miss Parker, and close the door." Marilyn Hawkins had a presence that seemed to demand respect, whether she had earned it or not. Faith wouldn't call her exactly intimidating, but she was certainly no shrinking violet. She stood ramrod straight, and when she spoke there was no doubt who was in charge. Her tone was...well, commanding.

"I wanted to talk to you about your classroom," she started, her voice filling up the room. "I know this is your first year and there are some things you'll have to learn with experience, but the other day when I came into your classroom, the children were out of control. We have a reputation to uphold here. Our parents expect us to be able to manage our classes. I'm sure you'll learn in time, if you're willing to take instruction from someone with experience. So I would like you to spend some time observing me on your conference period."

"Of course, Mrs. Hawkins. I'd be happy to do that. I would like to say, however, that—"

"I was afraid you would try to make excuses for the behavior of your children that day, and I know we all have our off days, but you really need to nip this in the bud."

"May I explain something? Tell you what the children were doing that day?"

"Of course. I'm listening." Faith wasn't convinced Mrs. Hawkins ever listened, but this was her chance to defend herself and she was going to take it.

"We were working on our ocean unit just like all the other kindergarten classes. They had just finished watching some videos I found on life in the ocean. When you walked in, each person was telling one fact he or she had learned. They were a little excited about the lesson."

"A little?" Marilyn Hawkins raised an eyebrow.

Faith took a deep breath and let it out slowly. "I'm sorry. I'll tell them to talk more quietly next time."

"A lot more quietly. Or maybe not at all. They have to recognize you as the authority figure in the classroom. Otherwise, they will never respect you."

Respect? Faith had observed Mrs. Hawkins's students in the cafeteria and on the playground when Marilyn was around, and she knew the difference in respect and fear. Those children didn't respect their teacher; they feared her. That was painfully obvious to Faith.

"I know Carrie thinks a lot of you," she continued. "She overruled me by hiring you. But I don't want to have to put you on probation if you can't get your class under control. I'll be walking in periodically, and I expect to see order the next time."

So that was it. Round One to Mrs. Hawkins. But Faith hoped she'd won only the first battle...not the war. "And that's what you'll see, Mrs. Hawkins," she conceded, as she tried to regulate her breathing and gain her composure.

"And I want you in my classroom during your planning time three days a week for the next two weeks, observing an experienced teacher. I'm sure you'll admit you still have a lot to learn."

"Yes, ma'am. I know I do. And I'm thankful for the opportunity to teach here. May I sit in on your class from ten to ten-thirty Monday?"

"I'll be expecting you. That will be all for today. Please close the door on your way out."

So Marilyn hadn't wanted to hire her in the first place. Faith wasn't surprised, but she was glad to know her principal wanted her...enough to overrule Marilyn. That was a comfort.

Faith stepped out of the shower, wrapped a thick white bath towel around her body, and rubbed her long auburn hair with another one. As she dried off, her thoughts were on her impending...they *were* calling it a date, weren't they? It had all the makings of a date: dinner, stroll along the harbor, no eleven-year-old chaperon. Faith remembered how careful Josh had been not to hurt Daniel's feelings, not to let him think he wasn't wanted. And Daniel had bought it—hook, line, and sinker. In fact, several times Daniel had let Faith know he was happy she and Josh were going out. Anything Josh did was okay with Daniel. And that was important to Faith, too. At least she and Josh agreed on one major thing: Daniel was special to both of them. Was that enough to base a relationship on, though? *Well, at least it's a start,* she concluded. It was more of a connection than she and Trent had at first. And she'd have to admit it was maybe more than they had now.

She'd been thinking for a couple of days about what to wear. "Dress up," he'd said. How dressed up? He wouldn't tell her where they were going—just that it was a restaurant on the harbor. Faith had developed quite an affinity for lobster since she'd moved to Maine. She hadn't eaten it often, but once when she'd gone to Lobster Bistro to see Annie Culwell, they'd split a lobster dinner when Annie's shift was over. As they had eaten, Annie'd tried to talk Faith into getting an apartment with her.

"I think we'd make great roommates, don't you?" she kept asking as they cracked lobster claws.

Faith, not wanting to hurt her feelings but preferring to stay with her parents for the time being, had put her off.

"I'm sure you'd make a great roommate, Annie, but I want to wait until I've worked for a while longer and have some money saved up."

"Wow. You sound just like my sister, Maggie. You should meet her."

"I think I've seen her with you at church. She's older, right?"

"Yeah. She and Tracy Ratcliffe—I mean, Tracy Norsworthy—are good friends. Maggie would just as soon live at home and work at that little bookstore of hers for the rest of her life. I mean, it's not really hers, but it might as well be. Bernard lets her run it these days. I love my sister, but I don't get her at all."

These two sisters were as different as night and day, yet they seemed genuinely fond of each other. "I'll keep the apartment thing in mind, Annie. Maybe next summer if you still want to do it and I'm ready…" she conceded. "But in the meantime if you find someone else, don't feel bad about it. I can't guarantee anything right now." She couldn't guarantee anything about anything anymore. Not where moving out was concerned. Not where Marilyn Hawkins was concerned. Not where Trent was concerned. The only thing she was sure about was her excitement to be spending the evening alone with Josh.

Chapter Thirteen

The inside of Milo's Seafood House was dimly lit with dark, highly polished wood paneling, beveled windows that showcased the lights of the harbor, and velvet-cushioned booths with elaborately carved tables. Josh had reserved a booth in the back corner by the window and took Faith's hand as they followed the hostess.

"This is lovely, Mistah Butlah," Faith said, looking out at the harbor lights and the moored boats. "Ah didn't know they had anything like this in the North."

"Just wait, Miss Scarlet, until you taste the lobster. It'll put all this beauty to shame."

During dinner Faith told Josh about her run-in with Marilyn Hawkins, eliciting from him advice on how he felt she should handle the situation. On the one hand, she'd been brought up to respect authority, and Marilyn was her immediate supervisor. On the other hand, she couldn't change her teaching methods if she thought it would be to the detriment of her students.

She'd had this same discussion with Trent a few nights ago, and he'd surprised her with his response. "This is a new job, Faith. I don't think you should make waves. Just do what she says. What does it matter anyway how you teach if you lose your job?" What did it matter indeed? What did it matter if her students were afraid to come to school every day? What did it matter if their first year in school totally turned them off to learning? Faith had tried to explain her position, but Trent didn't seem to understand.

Josh interrupted her thoughts. "I wouldn't expect you to be anything but respectful of authority, but I think you should fight, in a tactful way of course, for what you think is right for your students." He paused. "I don't know that I'm one to be handing out advice to anyone, though, especially you. I haven't always made good choices. Choosing not to practice law...yes. Some other choices I've made...well, let's just say I'm not someone you want to emulate."

"You've certainly made one little boy very happy for the past couple of months."

Josh had been feeling guilty about starting to work with Daniel for the wrong reasons and had been thinking about telling Faith the truth, hoping she would be able to see that although his initial motive wasn't entirely charitable, he wouldn't change a thing now. Daniel had become important to him, too. "Faith, I'm going to tell you something that I probably shouldn't...on a first date anyway. But I'm tired of playing games with my life. I'm gonna just put it out there. That okay with you?"

Faith's stomach churned. She wasn't sure she wanted to hear what Josh was about to say. Thinking she might have an idea what it was and having conflicted emotions about that made her feel she should keep him and his confessions at bay. "Why would you have to ask? That makes me think I might *not* want to hear it."

"Sure. No problem. See what I mean. I don't always make good choices."

"No one makes the right choices a hundred percent of the time. I know I don't."

"I have a hard time believing that."

"Well, it's true."

"Are you sorry you left Texas?"

"Oh no. I have total peace about that decision. Others I'm not so sure about, though."

"Then I guess we have that in common, don't we? Although I doubt any of what you call questionable choices could hold a candle to my questionable choices."

"What's this? A competition?"

"No. Just want you to know who you're having dinner with. You know…there are Saturday Night Girls and Sunday Girls, and you're a Sunday Girl. I don't think I've gone out with a Sunday Girl since I was in high school."

"And I don't think I've ever heard those terms before."

"They're Josh Whitehall-isms. That's probably why. Not really sure how to explain them to you, but I guess they're pretty self-explanatory."

"Then I'm going to take that as a compliment."

"As you should. Is your lobster good?" Josh asked, moving them on to a safer subject. If there was one thing he didn't want to do, it was blow his chances of another date with Faith Parker.

Faith dabbed at both corners of her mouth with her white cloth napkin. "Can't you tell by the lemon butter sauce that just threatened to run down my chin? It might be the best I've ever had. Did you know I'd never tasted lobster or clam chowder till we moved here?"

"Do you feel fulfilled now?"

"Well, I'm definitely feeling filled."

"We're having dessert, you know."

"Yeah? I don't usually turn down dessert. I hope you have something in mind because I don't want to have to make a decision."

"You like chocolate?"

"I'm a girl, aren't I?"

Oh yeah. You're definitely a girl. "What is it with girls and chocolate anyway?"

"I have a couple of friends who don't like it, but I'm thinking of unfriending them," she said, smiling, glad she'd been around Josh often with Daniel and felt comfortable with him. "So. What are we having?"

"Chocolate molten lava cake. I promise you'll like it…but…if you don't, you get to pick our next date destination."

"Our next date. Hmmm. Kind of presumptuous, aren't we?"

"How could you resist this smile," he asked. And there was that lopsided grin again.

How indeed?

"You know, Josh, I think we might need to talk before we go out again."

"Isn't that what going out is all about? Talking?"

"You know I'm dating someone."

"Yeah. Me."

She'd have to admit he did have a way of catching her off guard, of making her smile despite herself. "Okay. We'll postpone that talk until later, but we have to have it."

"I didn't mean to make light of what you have to say. Sorry if it came across that way. We can talk any time you want to. Now if that's what you want."

"No. I'm having a wonderful time. Let's just enjoy the rest of the evening."

"Me, too. That's why it makes perfect sense to do this again. Well, not this exactly. But something."

"Okay, mister, but what if I wanted to pick the next date destination even if I love the dessert? Are you a modern man or aren't you?"

"Well, if you put it that way—"

"Good."

"So?"

"So?"

"Where are you taking me on our next date? See. I'm even modern enough to expect you to drive."

"Give me some time to think about it. Don't expect it to meet Milo's standards. You've set the bar pretty high here."

As they walked along the shoreline after dinner, Faith's eyes scanned the harbor and she was quiet for a long time. When she finally spoke, it was almost with a kind of reverence. "This is beautiful. So different from the Dallas skyline. It's amazing what a body of water can do for somebody's mood. I never thought I'd live in a place where in only a few minutes, I could be standing on the edge of the Atlantic Ocean."

Faith's thoughts were concentrated on the boats and lights of the harbor. Josh's thoughts were on her. He'd never known anyone like this girl standing beside him. She was all at once soft but strong, kind but determined, fun but serious. And to think he'd been on the brink of spoiling what was to him a perfect evening with the confession that he agreed to meet with Daniel originally only to get to know her better. What was he thinking? Obviously she wasn't ready for that. She might never be ready. There was, after all, a guy in Texas who apparently still mattered to her. And they were going to have a talk about this Trent person.

"You know what I'd like to do sometime?" Faith asked, interrupting his thoughts.

"What's that?"

"I'd like to go sailing."

Faith had often wondered what it would like to get on a boat and be steered by only the wind. To be at the mercy of breeze and waves. To lie back in a sailboat and let it take her out, closer and closer to the horizon.

After a few seconds of silence, Josh said, "I don't sail," and when Faith looked up at his face, there was that look again. The look she'd seen when her mom had asked him if he had any brothers or sisters. A faraway look. A sad look. A look that said, *This isn't something I want to talk about.*

So she decided to change the subject. "Oh. I have a better idea. Do you have a bike?" she asked, feeling the need to rescue him again.

His expression instantly relaxed. "Yes."

"Do you like to ride?"

"I do."

"What about a bike ride and a picnic? I'll cook."

"Works for me, Miss Scarlet. A week from today?"

"Perfect."

"Andy, it's Ted Cameron. Sally said you called this morning looking for a pediatric oncologist in the Portland or Boston area. What's going on with my buddy?" Dr. Cameron had taken care of Daniel not only the two years he was undergoing treatment for leukemia, but also had continued to monitor him until the Parkers moved to Maine. He promised to keep in touch and asked Andy to keep him apprised of Daniel's progress or let him know if there were any problems.

"Thanks for returning my call so soon, Dr. Cameron. He's been exhibiting some signs that have us worried, and we want to get him checked out as soon as possible."

"What signs?"

"Loss of appetite, fatigue, a couple of light bruises on his thighs."

"Don't panic. If he's still playing basketball, that could cause all these things."

"We're trying not to jump to conclusions, but we're worried. And we'd like to get him to a good doctor for a complete checkup. Wish you'd move up here."

"I've been there in the fall. Wouldn't take much to tempt me. I bet it's beautiful now."

"It is. But we miss our favorite doctor."

"And I miss my buddy and his family. Listen. I've done some checking, and I have a couple of names for you—one in Portland and one in Boston. They're both pediatric oncologists. I don't favor one over the other, so I'd go to the one that can get you in the soonest."

"Go ahead. I'm writing."

"There's a Dr. Janine Layton in Portland and a Dr. George Simmons in Boston. I'll transfer you to Sally and she can give you both numbers. Let me know which one you're seeing and when, and I'll send his records."

"I'll let you know as soon as we can get an appointment. Thanks for always being there for us. Daniel misses your teasing him. I hope this new doctor is able to establish that kind of rapport with him."

"Tell you what. As soon as you get an appointment, I'll make a phone call and talk with the doctor. Let her or him know what a great kid Daniel is."

"Emily and I would appreciate it. Thanks for your help. I'll be in touch—soon, I hope."

Faith grabbed her phone to answer as soon as she saw Josh's name pop up on her screen. It was 4:32 on Monday afternoon. She'd told him she usually got home about 4:30 every day. Interesting timing. "Hi, Josh. I just walked in."

"I know. I'm psychic. Remember?"

"You *did* tell me that. What's up?"

"Two things. First I want to know how your observation with the Wicked Witch of the West went today. Ooh. Alliteration. Are you impressed?" She was, in fact, doubly impressed since Trent hadn't inquired about her meeting.

"Dreadfully," Faith replied. "She's not that bad, though. I sat in on one of her classes for about thirty minutes today and I'll observe another one Wednesday. She's not actually mean to her students, but they seem afraid of her because she's just so rigid. They don't have any chances to let out their pent up energy. And you know kids. They have wiggles they need to get out. There's a lot more group work and moving around in my class, but that's what she doesn't like. I guess I have two choices—conform to her standards and stay out of trouble or keep teaching according to my convictions and get put on probation…or worse. I need this job. If I lose it, I might have to go back to Texas…and I don't really want to do that. I'm talking too much again, aren't I?"

"If I didn't want to know, I wouldn't have asked. Wait. Did you say you don't want to go back to Texas? Can I take that to mean you think about our next date constantly and couldn't stand the thought of missing it?"

"Ha! I have some ideas about where to go. Let me do a little more research. I'll get back to you. When did you want to go? Saturday?"

"Well, let's see. Do you think tomorrow's too soon?"

"Tomorrow?"

"Just kidding. I'm coming over to work with Daniel tomorrow night."

"Math or photography?"

"Both probably. He's becoming both a photography expert and a math whiz…but I'm sure it has nothing whatsoever to do with my tutelage."

"No. I'm pretty sure he gets all his talent from his sister. Well. Guess I'd better go see if Mom needs help with dinner. Want to eat with us tomorrow night? I'll make a—"

"Yes! Oh. Sorry. I meant to sound a little more 'hard to get.' I should have said, 'I'll have to think about it for about, oh, half a second. Hmmm. Let's see. Why, yes, yes, I think I would.'"

"Okay. Good."

"That is, if it's all right with your parents."

"You know it is. If I didn't ask you, they probably would. And I'll tell you tomorrow where we're going. Are you free Saturday afternoon?"

"Sure am. It's a date."

"I guess it is at that."

"See you tomorrow night then...Oh, Faith. Wait. I almost forgot the other thing I called about."

"What's that?"

"One of my friends at the magazine is a reporter named Harvest Moon Hansen."

"Seriously? You're expecting me to believe that?"

"It's a long story. I'll tell you later. Anyway, she's cool. You'll like her a lot. She might be the only other Sunday Girl I know besides you. Well, she told me today our editor assigned her a story on education in Maine. Primarily the first couple of years of school when students are learning the basics...reading and other basic skills. So...I had this idea. Want to hear it now? Or tomorrow night?"

"Sounds intriguing, but I think I'd better wait until tomorrow. Be prepared to tell me about that name, too. Harvest Moon? Gotta be a good story there."

"Oh, there is. I can't wait for you to meet her."

Chapter Fourteen

"Faith," Andy said when Daniel had gone upstairs after dinner. "Mom and I need to talk to you about something. Do you have a minute? We weren't going to mention it this soon, but we want you in the loop on this from the beginning. Sit down, sweetheart."

"Sure. I was just going to load the dishwasher. What's going on?"

"I can do that, honey. Don't worry about it tonight. But thanks," Emily said.

"Okay. What is it? You guys look serious. Is everything all right?"

"We hope so, but we talked to Dr. Cameron—"

"Dr. Cameron? Why did you call him?" Faith interrupted, her eyes widening.

"You know Daniel hasn't been eating as much lately and he seems tired most of the time. His basketball coach saw some bruises on his legs the other day and called us in to his office. We have to consider… everything, you know."

"I thought he was just tired from practice," Faith said, her voice lowering to almost a whisper, her hands grasping the arms of the chair.

Andy put a hand on his daughter's shoulder. "We hope that's what it is, but we have to know for sure."

"Of course. So what's next?"

"With Dr. Cameron's help we got an appointment with a pediatric oncologist in Portland for next Tuesday. That's pretty amazing considering we would have had to wait two months if he hadn't intervened on our behalf."

"Well, that's good anyway. Daniel doesn't know anything yet, does he? I think he would have said something to me if he did."

"No. We're going to tell him it's a routine physical. He doesn't have to know the doctor is an oncologist. We wanted you to know first."

"Dad. Come on. You know Daniel's smarter than that. That word 'oncologist' will be on the door of the office."

"I think she's right, Andy," Emily agreed. "He's not the same age he was when we first took him to see Dr. Cameron. He'll figure it out, and then he'll probably wonder why we kept it from him if there was nothing to worry about. We just have to be careful *how* we tell him."

"You two are the voice of reason tonight," Andy said. "Of course we do. I don't know what I was thinking."

"You were thinking he's just a little boy, Dad. And he is, of course. But he's a smart little boy and he's pretty intuitive. It's totally different from last time…when he was three. It's different for me, too. I was younger and didn't understand as much. I kind of wish I could go back in time and not know what I know now. Not know what will lie ahead if it's—"

"Let's don't get ahead of ourselves. Mom and I will tell him it's time for a checkup and Dr. Cameron recommended someone he trusts. You can be there, too, if you want."

"I'd better not. Don't want him to think we're having a family council meeting about something serious."

"Meanwhile, we'll pray," Emily said.

Andy reached out, took hold of her hand, and squeezed it tightly. "We will, Em. You're giving me a dose of my own medicine. That's what I'd tell someone who had a similar situation and came into my office for counseling."

"Y'all just let me know if there's anything I can do to help out more this time…if he has to take chemo again, I mean. I can keep the house running, Mom, if you need to be with Daniel a lot."

"We know that, honey, and we're thankful to have such a thoughtful daughter," Emily said, enveloping Faith in a hug.

"We are indeed," Andy echoed.

"Hey, y'all. I forgot to tell you I invited Josh for dinner tomorrow night. He was coming over anyway. That okay?"

"Coming over anyway? I can't tell which one of my children he's coming to see anymore." Andy grinned at his daughter.

"Dad! Not you, too."

"I suspect it's been both all along, Andy. Sure it's okay. I'll have to admit I'm growing rather fond of that young man. He has a good heart. I can tell. There's still something puzzling about him, though. Oh, Faith. There's so much going on I forgot to ask how your observation of Mrs. Hawkins's classroom went today."

"It was fine. I'm going back for another thirty minutes on Wednesday. Guess who did call to ask about it…and guess who didn't. Never mind. I'll tell you. Josh did and Trent didn't. I'll let you decide what that means."

"All that matters is what it means to *you*."

"And that's what I don't know, but I'll figure it out eventually. I'm going to spend all my emotional currency on Daniel right now. Let me know how he takes it when you tell him. I'm going up now. I'll look in on him."

"We will. Good night, sweetheart."

"Daniel Parker, Dr. Layton will see you now. Mom and Dad, you can come with him, of course."

"That's okay, guys. I got this," Daniel said, getting out of his chair with all the bravado of someone much older and less aware of what could be around the corner. The office had been full to overflowing when the Parkers walked in, but Daniel was one of the first ones to be called.

"He's an old soul, Em," Andy said after he'd left with the nurse. "What did we ever do to deserve him? Or Faith either, for that matter? Who could have asked for two better kids? One from your womb and one from the womb of a scared and confused fifteen-year-old girl. I wonder where she is now…Jenna. Do you ever think about her?"

"Almost every day. I wonder if she's married and has a family, if she still lives in Texas, if she thinks about her firstborn. I wonder if Daniel will want to find her when he gets older."

"How would you feel if he did?"

"Not threatened, if that's what you're asking. We're his parents and he's our son. We know that and I know he does, too. It would be natural if he decides to look for her some day. She let it be known she didn't want to be a part of his life in any way, but I wonder if she's changed her mind. If she would be happy to see what a fine boy he's grown into. In a few years, of course."

"During the whole ordeal, I couldn't keep from thinking that she was…is…just a few years older than Faith. She was so young when she was pregnant with Daniel."

"I'm still amazed when I think about how God orchestrated that whole thing," Emily said. "What would have happened to her if Teresa hadn't found her sitting on the steps of the church that day and brought her in to your office."

"How we'd been praying for another child, and it didn't look like it was going to happen. How we'd just started throwing around the word 'adoption.'"

"All of that. And I hope that by adopting Daniel we helped her make a good life for herself. I wish she'd wanted to stay in touch, though. I'd like to be able to send her pictures. Tell her what a wonderful kid he is. How happy he's made us. What a great little brother he's been for Faith. What an amazing older sister she's been to him."

"I think she probably knows that. We made it evident to her how much we wanted him and what kind of home and family we could give him. You know, Em, I believe that people come into our lives for a reason. Some stay with you for a long time and some leave soon. Even the ones who go quickly leave you with something, though, whether good or bad. And sometimes they come back. She knows how to get in touch with us if she wants to. And we haven't hidden it from Daniel that he was adopted and the circumstances...that his biological mother was young and unmarried and couldn't take care of him. If she ever *did* come back into our lives, I think he would take it well. He's always felt that she did him a favor by letting us adopt him."

Andy and Emily sat for what seemed like an interminable length of time, Emily looking at magazines and Andy working on his sermon for Sunday, before Dr. Layton walked into the waiting room. "Hello. You must be Reverend and Mrs. Parker. I'm Janine Layton. Won't you come back to my office? Daniel's getting dressed, and I'd like to talk to all three of you together."

The Parkers looked at each other, and Andy noticed that his wife was choking back tears.

"I feel," Dr. Layton continued, "and Dr. Cameron has confirmed, that Daniel is mature enough to sit in on this conversation, but of course that's your call."

"We'll go with whatever you think. Em?" Andy said, glancing at Emily. She nodded in agreement.

"Hey, buddy." Andy spoke when Daniel walked into the office, not sure whether Emily could.

"Dr. Layton is as cool as Dr. Cameron…maybe cooler. She likes basketball, and she might come see one of my games."

"Well, that *is* cool, isn't it?" Andy replied, realizing that Daniel wasn't aware of the seriousness of this meeting.

"Daniel's going to show me some of his photography next time, too. I hear he's been taking a lot of pictures since you all moved from Texas. How do you like our fall in New England?"

"Beautiful," Emily answered, regaining her composure and her voice. "So different from what we're used to."

"I've never regretted moving here from the Midwest." Janine Layton adjusted her position in her chair, as if she were trying to get more comfortable for the news she was about to deliver. "Guys, I'm going to want to do some more testing to be sure, but I can say with almost a hundred percent certainty that Daniel's leukemia has returned. Be assured that there are measures we can take to deal with it, and that we will pull out all the stops to do so. I won't sugarcoat it, and I know you're aware of some of the things involved, but I can tell that this young man is a fighter, and I will be in there all the way fighting alongside him. We'll send his labs off this afternoon, and they should be back in a couple of days. Meanwhile, I'd like him to continue with his activities as much as he feels like it. He tells me he's been getting tired at basketball practice. I'll write his coach a note if you think that would help."

"Thanks, Dr. Layton, but I don't think that will be necessary. Coach Miller is very understanding, and we'll explain the situation to him."

"Daniel tells me he has a game Thursday night. I'd like to come if that's okay with the three of you. I live in Kennebunk, so it's close for me."

"Sure. You'd like that, wouldn't you, Daniel?"

"That's cool. My sister and her boyfriend will be there, too...so you can meet them." Andy and Emily cut their eyes at each other with looks that said *What does he know that we don't?*

"I'd love to. I'll give you a call as soon as the lab results are in and let you know what's next. I'll also give Dr. Cameron a call to keep him in the loop. It was so nice to meet all three of you." Coming from behind her desk, Janine Layton shook Daniel's hand first, then Andy's and Emily's. "Keep on taking those great pictures. I'll want to see some soon."

"'My sister and her boyfriend will be there'? Do you know something we don't? Is Trent coming to Maine...or is there another explanation for that comment, buddy?" Emily was trying to suppress a laugh as they got in the car, thankful for something to talk about besides what Dr. Layton had just told them, although the news didn't come as a surprise to her.

"Yeah, Daniel. Where *did* that come from? Are you privy to some information we don't have?" his dad asked.

"What does that mean?"

"What does what mean?"

"That word you used. Privy."

"Oh. I was just asking if you have some kind of secret information that we don't have. And if Faith has told you something in confidence, that's okay. You don't have to tell us."

"She didn't tell me anything. I can just tell. I can tell Josh likes her a lot and I think she likes him, too. They're going on another date, and this time Josh said Faith can pick the place. That makes them girlfriend and boyfriend, doesn't it?"

"What about Trent? Where do you think he fits in?" Emily asked.

"I don't know, but one time when he was in Dallas and I was playing basketball he didn't want to see my game, so I hope she likes Josh better."

"Time will tell, I guess."

"I have a question," Daniel said.

"Shoot."

"Will I have to have chemo again?"

"We don't know for sure yet, son. Maybe, though."

"If I do, will I lose my hair like I did last time?"

"I guess it depends on the type of chemo you have to take. I think there are some kinds that don't cause you to lose your hair. Are you worried about that?"

"Not really. I bet if I lost my hair, I could wear a baseball cap at school, couldn't I?"

"Probably. We'd have to check with the principal, of course."

"That would be so cool."

Andy and Emily smiled at each other. There seemed to be no end to their son's optimistic view of life.

"Harvest Moon? Really?" Faith asked Josh the next time he was over to help Daniel with math. "What kind of parents name their daughter Harvest Moon? Or did she change it herself later?"

"Nope. That's the name her parents, who are actually her grandparents, gave her when she was two days old."

"Her grandparents are her parents and her real name is Harvest Moon. This just gets better and better. Tell all."

"Her grandparents were real, honest-to-goodness, Woodstock-attending, weed-smoking hippies, and well...I'll let her tell you the story when you two meet."

Faith realized she was going to have to drag this story out of Josh, but she didn't mind. It only meant she'd get to talk to him longer before he went upstairs to help Daniel. "Does she fit her name? Is she a modern-day hippie?"

"Whatever that is, huh?"

"Yeah. I guess I have a vision of what I think it is, but I'm not really sure either," Faith admitted.

"She's an awesome girl. Creative, strong-willed, principled. A lot like you."

"That kind of sounded like a compliment."

"Only because it was. I can't wait for you two to meet."

"When—and why—are you planning this meeting?"

"Okay. So you remember I told you she's a reporter for the mag and is doing a story on education? Do you think your principal would allow her to observe you and your classroom and include that in her story? She could focus on your teaching methods…and maybe even interview some of your students…ask them what they've learned this year? Prove the Wicked Witch of the West wrong? What do you think?"

"She'd have to go through Mrs. Randolph, of course, but it's all right with me. I wonder if it wouldn't be better for her to focus on Marilyn, though, since she's the kindergarten department head."

"That's just it. She would focus on both of you. She'd have to interview *her* students, too." It seemed that Josh had given this quite a bit of thought.

"I'm sure she'd have to obtain parent permission to interview our students and the parents might want to be present during the interview, but I think some of my parents would be fine with it. I have a lot of moms who are very involved in volunteer work at the school, and I've gotten to know them pretty well."

"Cool. I'll tell Harvest to get in touch with the principal. Could I give her your number, too?"

"Of course. I'd love to meet her."

"Good. I'll go see Daniel now. He's probably wondering where I am."

"Could you stay another minute? I need to talk to you about something else."

"Is this that 'talk' we were going to have?" Josh asked, beginning to feel uneasy. "I'm not sure I'm ready for that."

"It's not *that* talk, but it's important. And as an honorary member of the Parker family, which my parents say you are, it's something I think you need to know."

"Ooh. I get in on the Parker family secrets now. I'm honored."

"You might not feel so honored to hear this one. It's not a secret exactly, but we're not talking about it yet to other friends, so maybe you should feel honored in a way."

"You're killing me here. What's going on?"

"I don't think I told you that Daniel had leukemia when he was three, did I?"

"I don't think I like where this is going."

"We don't know for sure yet, but you know how he's been getting tired a lot lately?"

"Yeah. He hasn't been himself for a while. I've noticed that."

"Mom and Dad took him to a doctor, and she thinks the cancer has returned."

"No. Don't tell me that, Faith. I can't—" Josh looked away shaking his head. "I just can't—"

"I know. We can't believe it either."

"I mean…What I mean is… Dan… Daniel can't—" he stammered and pounded his fist on the kitchen counter.

"I know, Josh. I can't stand the thought of it for him either if he has to go through all that again. He was so sick last time."

"Does he know?" Josh asked after he'd partially regained his composure.

"He knows it's a possibility. In fact, he's been joking about being able to wear a cap to school if he loses his hair again."

"What a kid! He doesn't deserve this, you know."

"Don't mention it to him, but I didn't want you to be caught off guard if he says something about it to you. He was so young that he doesn't remember how sick he was."

"Sure. I understand. I'll let him tell me about it if he wants to. I think I'll go up now. Thanks for letting me in on it. I just—I can't—"

"I know."

Chapter Fifteen

"Reverend Parker. This is Dr. Layton. I have the results of Daniel's blood work, and I've talked to Dr. Cameron. Would you and your wife like to come in, or do you want to talk over the phone?"

"This is fine. You can tell me and I'll let Emily know."

"As I suspected, Daniel's acute lymphoblastic leukemia has returned. Be assured that I, along with my team of specialists, will be aggressive in dealing with this. Of course, we'll start with a bold chemotherapy protocol. I've already consulted some experts in the field of ALL recurrence and will be working with them throughout the treatment. You know, of course, that life as you and Mrs. Parker know it now will change for a while. Dr. Cameron has assured me that Daniel is a spunky little fighter. I found him to be delightful. I have every hope and expectation that we will beat this thing. Do you have any questions for me now?"

"Just one at this time, but I'm sure after I talk with my wife I'll have more. She'll think of things that would never enter my mind. What's our next step?"

"We want to get the chemo started as soon as possible, but the first step is installing the port. I noticed he had one last time. This one can go in the same place. Let me switch you back to Carol, and she'll schedule your first appointment. We can do the chemo as an outpatient unless he's not tolerating it well. If that happens, he'll be hospitalized for a couple of days per treatment. The appointments will be in Portland. I'll get you to Carol now, but please feel free to call if you think of any other questions."

"Thank you, Dr. Layton."

Andy left work early, telling his secretary he had some family matters to attend to. He wasn't ready to announce to the community that Daniel would be undergoing chemotherapy because he knew people would start calling to see how they could help and arriving at their door with pies and casseroles. It was a nice problem to have. These were the deep-rooted connections that bound communities together, and in time he and Emily would appreciate the help. But for a day or two he wanted this to be something shared by only their family.

"You're home early." Emily eyed her husband suspiciously as he walked into the kitchen. "Dr. Layton called, didn't she?" she asked, feigning a nonchalance she didn't feel.

"She did," Andy answered, putting his arms around his wife, hidden tears choking his voice back. He already knew how she would react. She would do what she always did in a crisis. She'd find out what needed to be done and she'd set out to do it.

"When do we start the chemo?" she asked, her chin trembling and her throat tightening.

"Carol scheduled the first treatment for a week from Friday. He'll get his port on Monday."

"When should we tell him?" Emily's tears were not so hidden. They ran freely down her cheeks now, this mother who'd been through chemo with her son before and knew better than anyone what lay ahead. Knew about the nights when he'd wake up with cold sweats and have to be rocked back to sleep. She wondered if he was too old to be rocked back to sleep now. He seemed older than eleven in many ways, but she knew when he was sick with fever and nausea, he'd be her little boy again and she'd yearn to have him crawl up in her lap so that she could sing away his fever and his fear.

Andy handed her his handkerchief and she dabbed at her eyes. "Tonight, don't you think? I don't see any reason to put it off."

"I think you're right. Should I call Faith? She's out of class by now."

"I'll do that, Em. But I'm going to tell her not to mention it to Daniel when she picks him up. He needs to be home when he hears it...in case he's not quite as brave as he seemed the other day."

"Maybe Faith should be here, too. Let's wait to tell them both after dinner tonight. Faith first and then Daniel."

"That might be best. She told Josh the other night, didn't she? About the possibility, I mean."

"Yes."

"Do you think we should call him to come over?"

"Let's leave that up to Faith. They seem to have some kind of understanding...or something. I'm really not sure what's going on there. Do you have any idea?"

"No. But I trust our daughter completely to get it right. Whether it's Trent or Josh or someone totally different...or no one at all. She'll make the right decision."

"You know what's ahead of us, don't you? Six years hasn't been long enough to forget what we went through." Emily would never forget it and she knew her husband wouldn't either, but he could get away to his study, close the door and shut out the world. That was a luxury that she, as a mother and primary caregiver, didn't have.

"I do, but we handled it then and we'll handle it now. Faith is older now and can help more. She wasn't driving when we started on the journey last time."

"I guess I was referring to the emotional journey. The last time Dr. Cameron assured us that the chemo would do its thing and wipe out the cancer, so even though we hurt for Daniel when he was sick and juggling schedules was hard, we always had it in the back of our minds that he would live. But what about a recurrence? Did Dr. Layton say anything like that to reassure us?" Emily asked, the tears once again beginning to flow.

"What she said was that she'll be working with a team of specialists and that they will be treating it aggressively. You know, Em, every day advances are made in treating diseases like this. It's been eight years since he was first diagnosed and six years since his last treatment. Can you imagine how much more doctors know about the disease and treatment now than they did then? We need to be hopeful…for Daniel's sake…for our sakes."

"I'm hopeful, Andy, but that's my little boy. He didn't come from my womb, but I'm the one who rocked him to sleep at night and kissed him and bandaged his cuts when he fell down. But I shouldn't expect you to always be the strong one. I'm going to take a step back and a deep breath and prepare myself for what's to come. And I'll try to remember that God loves him even more than we do. There's a reason Jenna didn't choose to have an abortion. I believe God has great things in store for our son, and there's a reason he's in our family."

Andy texted Faith to come back downstairs after she'd helped her mother with the dinner dishes and gone upstairs for the night. "What is it?" She looked from one parent to the other. "We got the results of the blood test?"

"Dr. Layton called. Daniel's leukemia has returned. She'll start him on an aggressive chemo protocol next week," her dad said.

"I suspected that. I guess I braced myself for bad news. Poor guy. Just when he was rocking his new school and his basketball team. Remember what I said, Mom. Don't worry about the house. I can do the cooking and the cleaning while you spend all the time you need with Daniel."

"I appreciate your willingness, but you have a fulltime job now. We'll share the household chores and if the house gets a little dirtier than normal, then so be it."

"Never thought I'd hear you say that, Em," Andy said, "but you're right. Besides…there are two adults living here besides you. We can all pitch in."

"I know. We'll get through it. It won't be easy, but we *will* get through it. I hope Daniel's new friends will rally around him like Mitch and Lucas would have if this had happened in Dallas."

"I guess we need to tell Josh, don't we?" Faith asked.

"Could we count on you to do that, Faith?"

"Sure, Dad. But he took it harder than I thought he would when I told him it was a possibility. I honestly thought he was going to cry. I think he got mad just to *keep* from crying."

"They've developed a special bond, haven't they? And I wouldn't be surprised to find out it's been as good for Josh as it's been for Daniel."

Faith cringed as she dialed Josh's number. This was not a call she was looking forward to making. She'd rather call Trent and tell him. He wasn't as close to Daniel. It wouldn't affect him as much. Josh, on the other hand, well…she'd seen something she didn't like in his reaction the night she told him about the doctor's appointment.

Sadness maybe? But it was more than that. She saw that same faraway look he'd had when Emily had asked him about brothers and sisters and when she'd mentioned sailing. Same vacant stare. He hadn't responded immediately, and when he did he wasn't convincing. Her mother had summed it up. He was a mystery man, but he was a mystery man with a good heart.

He answered immediately. "Hey! You ready to tell me where we're going Saturday?"

"No." Faith took in a long, deep breath. "I mean I haven't totally decided yet."

"This call isn't about our date, is it?"

"No. It's not."

"It's back, right?"

"It's back."

They sat for a moment, neither one speaking. What was there to say at a time like this? Finally, Josh recovered enough to ask, "What can I do, Faith? I should be the strong one here since I'm not really family…but I'll admit I don't feel as strong as you sound right now."

"Probably the best thing you can do for Daniel—for Mom and Dad, too—right now is keep doing the same things you've been doing. We're going to try to keep his life and his activities as normal and stable as possible. That won't be easy because he'll be sick a lot and have to miss some school."

"I can continue to help him in math. I'm not too shabby in science and history, either. English, well, that's another matter."

"I don't know about that. You slipped when you used the term 'alliteration' the other day, so I'm not sure I believe that."

"An anomaly, I assure you. No. You'll have to take the reading and writing shift. When do his chemo treatments start? That's what they'll do first, isn't it?"

"He's going to a hospital to get his port installed Monday, and I think Mom said the treatments start a week from Friday. The doctor thinks if he has chemo on Friday, he might be able to go back to school on Monday."

"Sounds like a good plan. I hope it works. What's a port?"

"That's a small opening in his chest for a catheter that connects to a large vein so he doesn't have to get stuck every time he has an IV or has to have blood drawn. He had one last time. Makes everything so much easier."

"Oh. That's good. So how does he feel about not being able to play basketball anymore this season?"

"He'll still be on the team, still be sitting on the bench...kind of like he was before. Coach Miller's been great. He told Mom and Dad Daniel's a morale booster for the other guys. He manages to pump them up for the game even though he knows there's a big chance he won't get to play."

"Do you want to cancel our plans for Saturday? Do you feel like you should be with him?"

"Do you think that's what Daniel would want?"

"No. I don't get that feeling, do you?"

"No."

"He's made it pretty clear to me he doesn't mind being odd man out sometimes. Here's one thing I'm going to do...and don't try to talk me out of it. Every day Daniel has a chemo treatment I'm bringing dinner over."

"You're cooking?"

"Ha! You know better than that, but I am quite adept at calling ahead and picking up. Chinese, Italian, burgers, seafood...You name it. It'll be there by six."

"That's so nice of you."

"How many times have I eaten at your house?"

"I've lost count."

"I have, too, so now it's my turn. You want to pick the menu now or closer to the day?"

"Burgers would be great. Something we all like. Mom and Dad will appreciate it, I know. I'll tell them."

"Great. I'll have it there by six that day if that's okay."

"Speaking of...I need to go help Mom with dinner now. I'll pick you up at eleven Saturday. Have your tires aired up. I can get both bikes in the back of my SUV if I put the back seats down."

"I'm looking forward to our adventure, Miss Scarlet."

"Me, too. Bye."

"Hey, Faith. Thanks for calling to tell me about Daniel. Not a call I wanted to get, but it's always fun to talk to you."

"Not one I wanted to have to make either, but yeah...me, too."

Chapter Sixteen

After getting off the phone with Faith, Josh pulled his car to the side of the road and got out to stretch his legs and clear his head. A magazine assignment had taken him to Boothbay Harbor, and Faith had called with the news about Daniel as he was on his way back to Portland. Now he just wanted to walk and think...or walk and *not* think. The return of Daniel's leukemia brought a rush of still-raw memories...memories of losing Jordan, his only brother. It couldn't happen to Faith, too. It just couldn't. It hurt too much, and he didn't want her to ache the way he had. The circumstances were different, but still. A loss affected the ones left behind forever.

And it wouldn't affect only Daniel's family. Josh himself felt inexplicably drawn to the boy with a big-brotherly bond he thought he'd never experience again. To lose once...well, he was learning to deal with it. But to lose twice...he didn't know if he *could* deal with that.

He trekked along a copse of trees, reminiscing on his first encounter with Faith and Daniel. What was it Jessica had told him about the art gallery deck where they met?

She got her first kiss there? Her uncle met his wife there last summer? It was a deck with a history? He'd better be careful if he went up there? At the time, he'd laughed off that warning, but now... Now he couldn't deny the fact that two people he'd met there only a few months ago had changed his life in ways he never dreamed possible.

Daniel Parker had managed to worm his way into Josh's life as only Daniel could.

And Faith. Well, he couldn't believe he was letting a Sunday Girl turn his heart upside down. But then there was that Trent guy in Dallas, and Josh didn't know exactly where he stood in the food chain of Faith's admirers. *Out of sight, out of mind.* He really hoped that adage proved to be true in this case.

Faith opened her email at school the next day and her heart sank. Mrs. Randolph had written to her and Marilyn Hawkins requesting a meeting with both of them after school. Her mind raced as she tried to think of what could be wrong, why the principal would want to meet with both of them. Faith had been observing Marilyn every time she was supposed to. Marilyn hadn't been back in her classroom to check up on her, hadn't complained of noise, and she hadn't put her on probation. She couldn't think of a thing she'd done wrong, but her fragile state since learning about Daniel's leukemia had her imagining all kinds of possible problems. She zipped an answer back to the principal telling her she'd be there and went to stand at the door to wait for her morning students. Their smiles and hugs always brightened her day.

Hannah called from across the hall, "How's your brother doing, Faith? Is he handling the news well? And how are your parents?"

"Everyone's doing pretty well. Thanks for asking. I don't know if already going through this seven years ago will make it easier or harder this time. Easier because we know what to expect. Harder because we don't know what to expect. Know what I mean?"

Hannah's smile conveyed understanding. "Will you let me know if there's anything I can do to help? I mean that. If you need to take off early or come in late sometime, I can combine our classes for a while. That wouldn't be a problem at all."

Faith walked across the hall to stand next to her friend. "I really appreciate that. And I might have to take you up on it. I know Mom will want to be with him all the time, but she'll need to get away some, too. Dad and I might have to drag her away and we'll do that if necessary. It's a relief to know you're available if I ever need to leave early."

"Sure. I'm happy to help."

"Marilyn and I are meeting with Carrie this afternoon."

"What's that about?"

"I don't know. Got an email this morning."

"Can't be bad. You haven't done anything wrong. Keep me posted, though."

"Yeah. I will." Faith heard the outside door open and shrieks of laughter and excitement fill the hall.

"Here come our little angels. Just another day in paradise. Have a good one."

"You, too."

"Come in," Carrie called as Faith knocked lightly on the door of her principal's office. "Marilyn will be a few minutes late, but I'm glad you're here now. There's someone I want you to meet before she gets here."

As Faith entered, her eyes lighted on a dark-haired woman sitting to the right of the principal. Was she being fired and was this her replacement? Wouldn't she have been put on probation first? Carrie hadn't even talked to her about Marilyn's dissatisfaction with her classroom management.

No, she was almost certain this was the journalist Josh had told her about. Striking in appearance, the young lady was tall and slim with curly, shoulder-length hair and soft but piercing blue eyes. About Faith's age, she surmised. Her thoughts ran wild. Were she and Josh just friends? Had they ever dated? He'd spoken of her with admiration, but didn't mention a past relationship. Faith couldn't help but wonder, though.

"Faith Parker, Harvest Hansen. Miss Hansen is going to write a story for her magazine, *The Maine Way*, on the foundations of education in our state and would like to feature you as one of the teachers. Marilyn will be another one. I've read a couple of her stories, and I find her to be not only an excellent writer, but also a thorough and a fair journalist. She has my permission, but of course I want to get your okay, too, since you'll be spending some time with her and sharing your teaching methods and strategies. She will also need access to your classroom, and you'll have to see which parents will give written permission to have their children interviewed and photographed for the magazine."

Harvest stood and put out her hand. "It's so nice to meet you, Faith. My photographer, Josh Whitehall, will be documenting the article, and he's told me about you and your passion for teaching. I look forward to working with you."

Faith breathed a sigh of relief. So this wasn't her replacement. She wasn't in trouble. She was, instead, going to be featured in a magazine in Maine even though she'd lived here less than a year and been teaching only six weeks. And she supposed she owed it to one Josh Whitehall. Was this his way of allowing her to showcase her competence as a teacher? Then she would take full advantage of it. Bring it on, Harvest.

"Absolutely, I look forward to working with you. This is actually an honor. I would love to share my passion for teaching with you and your magazine."

Another knock on the door—this one not so light. Marilyn had arrived, and Faith wondered how she would take this turn of events. Instead of being on the hot seat, the new kindergarten teacher was going to be in the spotlight. They would *both* be in the spotlight, and she relished the idea of showing the magazine's readers that it was indeed possible to make learning fun and still maintain the respect of her students.

"So sorry I'm late, Carrie. I had a parent conference that lasted a little longer than I anticipated."

"Not a problem. Marilyn, this young lady is Harvest Hansen, with *The Maine Way* magazine. She's doing a piece on education, and I have given her permission to highlight you and Faith, your classrooms and teaching methods, that is. That means she'll do some interviews with you, and possibly some of your children, and will be sitting in on some of your classes. Are you comfortable with that?"

"Well, I...I'm—" Marilyn stammered.

"It's nice to meet you, Marilyn. I can assure you I'll be as unobtrusive as possible. The last thing I want to do is interfere with the daily routine in your classroom."

Had Carrie warned Harvest about Marilyn, Faith wondered. No, it must have been Josh. He was giving Faith a platform to show the world—well, *this* little corner of the world anyway—how her teaching methods compared to Marilyn's...and she was going to take full advantage of it.

"I suppose—"

"Thank you so much," Harvest jumped in before Marilyn had a chance to change her mind. "I'll be in touch with you both in the next day or two to set up a schedule for classroom visitations and interviews. And I'll have my photographer with me on a few of the visits. We'll need releases from parents who don't mind having their children's photos appear in the magazine, so if you'll both take care of that, I'd appreciate it. Here's a release form for each of you. You can make as many copies as you need."

"No problem, Harvest," Faith said. "I look forward to working with you on this project, and I thank you—and you too, Carrie—for the opportunity. I can just imagine how excited my kids will be when they see themselves in a magazine photo. That'll make their kindergarten year even more memorable."

"I appreciate your spirit of cooperation and your positive attitude, Faith," Carrie commented.

"So do I. It was nice to finally meet you after hearing so much about you from Josh. Nice to meet you, too, Marilyn," Harvest added.

Round Two to Faith. Well, now they were even.

Chapter Seventeen

"That's sweet of you, Trent, but totally not necessary. I'm fine." Faith had finally told him about Daniel's leukemia, and he'd surprised her with the announcement that he was planning to come to Maine in the next week or two...whenever he could take a long weekend.

"You don't *want* me to come?" he asked. Was that *hurt* she detected in his voice?

"It's not that. I don't want you to jeopardize your new job by asking off. I know how much it means to you."

"You mean more to me than my job does. How about that?"

"That's nice to hear," she reassured him, "but I just wanted you to know that if you wanted to wait and come later, when you've been working there longer, that's okay, too."

"I've never seen New England in the fall. Is it as pretty as everyone says?"

"Prettier. Pictures don't do it justice. You have to see it in person."

"And that's what I plan to do. I'll let you know tomorrow when I can come. Are there any hotels in Wentworth Cove or will I have to go to a larger city?"

"You couldn't exactly call it a hotel, but there is a small inn here. I could text you the name and number."

"Yeah. Do that."

I think Josh and I will have to have that talk after all, Faith concluded when the call ended. *And I think it'll have to be sooner rather than later.*

Since they were staying close to Wentworth Cove Saturday, Josh had talked Faith into letting him meet her at her house with his bike in the back of his Jeep. They could then put both bikes in her car and be off to wherever she was planning to take him. It was their second date, and he planned to make it memorable.

"Hey, Josh!" Daniel greeted his mentor as Josh pulled up in the Parkers' driveway. "Faith's still working on the food for the picnic. Wanna shoot some hoops before she gets ready?"

"Sure, buddy. I'll take you on for a few minutes. I don't want to get too tired, though. You wouldn't want me to let a girl outdo me on a bike ride, would you?"

"Nah. Don't worry about it, though. Faith's a good cook, but you're probably a better bike rider."

"Good to know. That might be embarrassing. Kind of like I'm embarrassed that you're beating me at this one-on-one right now."

"Okay. You'd better save your strength. Want me to tell her you're here?"

"Would you do that while I get my bike out?"

"Faith! Josh is here. Are you ready for your date?" Josh heard Daniel call at the top of his lungs as he ran into the house. It was so good to see him with this much energy, but Josh knew in a couple of weeks things would be much different.

"Still not going to tell me where we're going?" Josh asked when they were on their way.

"Nope." Faith headed north on Winter Harbor Road, passing trees cloaked in every shade of maroon, red, orange, and yellow. Admiring the vibrantly colored foliage, they rode in comfortable silence for a couple of minutes before she said, "Hey, I met your friend from the magazine at school yesterday."

"Harvest Moon? What do you think of her?"

"She's very pretty."

"She is, isn't she?"

"Seems nice."

"I had a feeling you two would hit it off. I heard she got permission from your principal to do the article."

"I don't think Marilyn is very happy about the whole thing, but I look on it as an opportunity to defend my teaching methods without being put on the defensive by her. Thank you for setting it up."

"Happy to help. Also happy to have you in my debt."

"Let's don't get carried away here. I said 'Thank you.' Not 'I'm in your debt.'"

"Deep down in that fair and just soul of yours, you know you are, though."

"What's it gonna cost me?"

"I'll think of something. For now, I'll file it away, pull it out when I need a favor, Miss Scarlet."

"You *do* know I'm from Texas, not Atlanta, don't you?"

"Anything south of Philadelphia is the Deep South to us Bostonians." Faith laughed as they continued toward their destination. She put the car windows down to revel in the crisp, clean air of a Maine October. She'd always liked fall in Texas, with its lower temperatures easing the pain of a scorching summer. But October in New England smelled of ripening apples, cool sea air and at times, on chilly evenings, smoke billowing from chimneys.

"We're going to Goose Rocks Beach, aren't we?" Josh surmised as they turned east toward the ocean.

"We are. I fell in love with it when you brought Daniel and me here. Been wanting to come back for a long time. Do you remember that park with the riding trails? I thought we could have our picnic there and then ride. Did you bring your camera?"

"No. I left it in my car. This is a date, not work."

"Did you lock your car?"

"No. We're in small-town Maine, not big-city Texas."

"But still…"

"If it'll make you feel better, I'll call Daniel and tell him to take it in the house."

"Good idea."

Faith pulled the car into a parking spot when they arrived at their destination.

"Uh, Faith…"

"Yes, Josh?"

"I think you have to have a parking sticker to park here. Remember when we came last time? I stopped and bought a sticker at the Chamber of Commerce?"

"Actually, I do remember that, and that's probably why I drove over here a couple of days ago and procured one. Voila!" she said, producing it from her purse and handing it to him. "Want to put it on the car window for me?"

"You're quite the planner, aren't you? I'd be happy to. Pop the back door. I need to get something out."

Walking around to the back of the car, Josh reached for the bouquet of yellow mums, bottle of water, and vase he'd hidden there after loading his bike. He handed the flowers to Faith. "I did a little planning ahead, too. Couldn't find any yellow roses, that Texas thing, you know. Will yellow mums do?"

"Oh! That's so sweet. I love them."

"Here. I'll spread the quilt and put the flowers in the middle."

"Thank you. They're lovely, Josh. Better for this time of year than roses anyway."

As Faith emptied the picnic basket and set the quilt "table," Josh put the sticker on the car windshield.

"Do I smell fried chicken?"

"Fried chicken, potato salad, corn on the cob, and pecan pie. Is that Southern enough for you, Mistah Butlah?"

"Homemade fried chicken?"

"Of course."

"People make fried chicken at *home*?"

"Some people do. Mom and I do."

"Let's quit talking about it and dig in."

They ate in relative silence, talking only occasionally about mundane things, both of them staying away from Daniel's illness and Faith's ongoing problems with Marilyn Hawkins. Faith decided it was time to have the Trent talk, though. Better now since they were in a relaxed setting and away from home.

"You know that talk we were going to have?" she asked.

"Do we really want to do this right now?"

"I might not want to, Josh, but I have to."

"You do?"

"I do."

"Okay."

"I'll just throw it out there. I told Trent about Daniel, and he's decided to come to Maine for a few days."

"Let's see. Trent. Trent. You've mentioned him before, I think. One of your old childhood friends, right? He's married with eight children, isn't he? It will be nice to meet a friend of the family."

"You know exactly who I'm talking about, and you know why I'm telling you."

"You haven't told him about us, have you?"

"What does that mean, 'about us'?"

"That we're dating…"

"No. I haven't told him."

"Hmmm. I wonder what that can mean. I know about him, but he doesn't know about me. I can spin it two ways. One, you don't want him to know you're dating me because you don't plan to keep dating me so why muddy the water. Or, two, you find me easier to talk to and you know he's not very understanding. I pick number two."

"You sound pretty confident."

"Not at all confident. But very hopeful."

"Look, Josh. I haven't seen Trent since June. Well, except for FaceTime, but that doesn't count. I'll admit to being a little confused right now. I didn't ask him to come. That was his idea. But we *have* dated for over a year, and we have a history."

"*We* have a history. We met on the deck at Norsworthy Art Gallery. And if you don't know what that means, just ask Jessica. It's noteworthy."

"Well, I thought you deserved to know."

"I appreciate that. I really do. When will he be here? I'll stay out of sight, but I hope not out of mind."

"You can't exactly stay out of sight."

"Why not?"

"Because he'll be here when you bring the hamburgers next Friday. And I've already told Daniel and my parents that you're doing that. You don't want to disappoint a little boy after his first round of chemo, do you?"

"When you put it like that… I'll just drop them off and leave, though. That will make it easier."

"I thought we were going to keep things normal for Daniel."

"Yeah. I just thought—"

"I'm sure he'll expect you to stay and eat with us. Will you, please? For him?"

"If that's what you want. Do I have to buy the cowboy's hamburger, too?" Josh asked, raising his eyebrows. "Just kidding. Of course, I will. Does he take arsenic or strychnine with his burger? Oops. Freudian slip. I meant mustard or mayonnaise."

No matter how serious the topic of conversation, Josh could always make her laugh. "The cowboy? I find it amusing the way people up here think of Texas. You should go to Dallas sometime. We have freeways to rival I-95 and skyscrapers to rival...well, there's really nothing here for them to rival. Anyway, don't expect Trent to arrive wearing cowboy boots and spurs. He might even still have on a suit and tie if he works half a day and goes straight to the airport."

"Maybe I should dress up then. I'll see what I can come up with."

"Don't look on this as a rivalry, Josh. I just want us all to be there for Daniel. He'll probably be feeling tired even if the nausea doesn't hit for a day or two. Let's make it a pleasant evening for him."

"Absolutely. Don't worry. I'll be a total gentleman. I'd do just about anything for that kid. You know that."

"I do. And I appreciate it. Want some more pie?"

"No, thanks, but it was delicious...as usual."

"Ready to ride?" Faith asked as she took the mum bouquet out of the vase and poured out the water. "I think I'll put these in my bicycle basket. Might as well enjoy them to the fullest."

"Let's do it. I'll help you put the food away and then get the bikes out of the car."

The ride along the coastline of Goose Rocks was relaxing but invigorating as the bracing sea air and an autumn slant of light more subtle in its illumination than the harsher light of summer beckoned them to the far end of the beach. Once there, they parked their bikes and walked toward the water. Josh took Faith's hand as he had on their first date when they had strolled along Portland Harbor.

He hadn't kissed her that night, but he would rectify that today. And the beach was the perfect place, he assured himself. They were in a place she loved, and even though Trent had been a topic of conversation earlier, he felt sure she would be receptive if he didn't overplay it. Just a slight one. His lips brushing against hers, a sort of prelude of what the future could hold for them.

Faith broke the silence. "I know you've had this your whole life, but it's still new for me. I'm amazed at how different I feel when I'm standing at the edge of an endless body of water."

"I hope you appreciate the way I arranged high tide just as we got here."

"You know how I remembered to get that parking sticker?"

"Yeah."

"I checked the tide charts, too," she said, throwing her head back and laughing, obviously pleased with her ability to retain the top spot in the "planning" war.

"Oh, man. I can't claim credit for anything—"

"The flowers weren't my idea, and I love them. They're perfect for a perfect fall day."

"Whew. I did something right."

"You do lots of things right, Josh. Knowing you has made it easier not only for Daniel to adjust to life in a different place, but for me, too. I appreciate your friendship."

Friendship? The word wasn't exactly conducive to that kiss he had planned. Their relationship had certainly become more than that for him. From the first moment he brushed by Faith on the deck of the art gallery—saw her, touched her, smelled her—he'd been smitten. He did consider her a friend, but it didn't stop there. There was the matter of his heart, and as much as he might try to deny it, Josh Whitehall was falling in love with Faith Parker.

There was no turning back for him, and if he had to fight for her, he would...with every fiber of his being. He'd forego the kiss for today and assess the Trent factor when he met him on Friday, but when the urban cowboy was safely back in Dallas, he would pull out all the stops. He thought he was pretty good at reading people, and unless he was horribly mistaken, Faith felt something stronger than friendship for him, too.

Chapter Eighteen

Emily picked up the phone on the second ring. It was Thursday afternoon, and she'd been cleaning house all day. Trent was due in tomorrow, and even though he wasn't staying with them, she wanted the house to be spotless. Not that it wasn't usually spotless anyway, but staying busy was helping her pass the time and keep her mind off "The Return," as she and Andy had started referring to Daniel's relapse.

"Emily? Kate Norsworthy here. Tomorrow is the day for Daniel's first chemotherapy treatment, isn't it?"

"Yes, it is."

"How are you doing?"

"Fairly well. Hoping, of course, that the treatments work quickly and don't make him as sick as they did last time. How are you?"

"I'm fine. Listen. Some of our mutual friends, mostly members of the congregation, have been asking about what they can do to help, and I thought some meals would be nice. We could also run errands for you or sit with Daniel if you and Reverend Parker would like to get out sometime. I'd be happy to get this organized and be the contact person if that's agreeable to you."

"Kate, that's so kind. Let me see how it goes and talk to Andy about it...see what he thinks would be best. I know people are eager to help, and we'll probably take them up on it to a degree. Everyone's been so nice."

"I'd like to bring dinner over tomorrow night to start the ball rolling if that's okay."

"That's so sweet of you, but actually Josh is picking up hamburgers for us. Faith has a friend coming in from Dallas, so tomorrow might not be the best time, but I'm sure we'll appreciate it in the near future."

"Josh Whitehall? He and Daniel are still working together on photography? I just assumed, I guess, that after school started, Daniel would make some friends and Josh would ride off into the sunset. Not so, huh?"

"Not so at all. Josh has become a real mentor to him...almost like a big brother. He's helped him as much with math as he has with photography. I don't think we could ever pay him back, but he does eat with us a lot, and he seems to enjoy being with the whole family. I don't think he has a very close relationship with his parents. Nothing he's said really, but I get that idea."

"I'm glad to hear my matchmaking skills are still as sharp as ever."

"That's right. It *was* your idea, wasn't it? Since Jessica called to tell me he'd agreed to mentor Daniel, I'd forgotten you suggested getting them together in the first place."

"It seems to have worked well for both of them. I'm glad. I'll let you go, Emily. You probably have a lot to do to get ready for tomorrow. But will you please call me if you need anything? Anything. And I'll start signing up people for meals if you don't mind...maybe every three days or so?"

"That would be great. Thanks for taking care of fielding calls and organizing things. That alone will give me more time with Daniel."

As soon as Emily put the phone down, her son bounded down the stairs. Watching him, she didn't think he looked like a boy whose leukemia had returned. Today he looked like a normal eleven-year-old guy with limitless energy. Tomorrow would be a much different day, however. Tomorrow would be the end of life as she'd known it for six years of remission. Tomorrow would be the beginning of one of the hardest years of her life.

"Why is Trent coming to Wentworth Cove?" Daniel asked.

"I think he wants to see Faith. Don't you imagine that's why?" Emily had wondered, too, why he had chosen Daniel's first day of chemo to show up, but she assumed he and Faith had discussed it and her daughter was fine with the visit. But Trent and Josh in the same room? She wasn't sure how that would play out, but her money was on Josh.

"I don't think she wants to see him."

"No? Why don't you think she wants to see him?" Daniel seemed to know more about Faith and Josh than the rest of the family did.

"Well, she's dating Josh now. Duh. Why would she need *two* boyfriends?" Emily laughed. That was Daniel. Always the pragmatist.

"What makes you think Josh is her boyfriend? Did she tell you that?"

"She didn't have to. I just know. She likes him and he likes her, so if Trent comes tomorrow, it might mess things up."

"How could it mess things up?"

"Well, Josh might think she likes Trent better than she likes him, and he might quit taking her on dates."

"Would that bother you?" Emily asked. "If Josh and Faith quit going out?"

"Yeah."

"I like Josh, too, but we have to let Faith make up her own mind about who she wants to date or not date. Don't you think?"

"I guess, but if she picked Trent, she'd be making a big mistake…just so you know." Subject closed. As far as Daniel was concerned anyway.

"We'll just have to trust Faith to do the right thing and wait and see how it all works out, won't we?"

"Uh huh. What time am I going to the doctor tomorrow? And when will I start losing my hair? Mr. Cunningham said when it starts to fall out I can shave my head and wear a ball cap if I want to. Cool, huh?"

"Oh, definitely cool. I'm sure it will take a few weeks, though."

Faith walked into the room, and Emily was glad she'd heard only the last comment. "What will take a few weeks?"

"I get to wear a ball cap to school when I lose my hair, but Mom thinks it'll take a few weeks. Mr. Cunningham said when it starts to fall out I can shave my head and start wearing a cap."

"That's way cool. Your principal must be as great as mine is."

"He calls me Tex, and I think he likes to hear me talk. He always stops me in the hall and asks me how I'm doing. He did that before he knew about the leukemia. I guess he didn't think I could make friends fast, but I met Landon on the first day of school. He's the one who started calling me Tex, and then everyone else did, too. Hey, Mom. Is it okay if Landon comes over tomorrow night?"

"Sure. Why not? We'll make it a party. What time will Trent get here, Faith?"

"Around six or seven, I think, but it might depend on the traffic getting out of Boston. He's renting a car at the airport. Daniel, does Josh need to pick up a burger for Landon?"

"No. His dad's bringing him over at eight. He's just coming to bring my homework, but he might stay to play some video games."

"Mom, do you need any help getting things ready for tomorrow?" Faith asked.

"No, thanks, honey. I think I've got it covered since I don't have to cook when we get home from Portland. It was nice of Josh to offer to bring burgers. That will be a big help."

"He's a nice guy, *isn't he, Faith*?" Daniel yelled as he headed upstairs.

"Yes, he is. He's a very nice guy," Faith agreed as she turned to go back upstairs, too.

And Emily was left to wonder what kind of entertainment Friday night would bring to the Parker household.

Chapter Nineteen

At six o'clock sharp on Friday evening, Josh rang the Parkers' doorbell. Andy opened the door and almost passed out. Before him stood a young man dressed to the nines in clothes Andy didn't know Josh possessed. He'd never seen him in anything but the most casual of shorts and jeans, T-shirts and sweatshirts. He did have on khakis and a button-down white shirt when he picked up Faith for their first date, and Andy assumed that was as dressy as he got, but tonight was different. Josh's appearance left Andy momentarily speechless.

But the clothes weren't the only thing. Josh's long, sandy blond hair was gone, and in its place, a black baseball cap with a red B—a Boston Red Sox cap. Andy felt a lump forming in his throat. Emily was right. Josh had a big heart and was showing his love and support for Daniel in the best way he could think of.

Daniel, who was rarely ever speechless, called from the den, "Hey, Josh. I'm in here."

Having regained his composure, Andy spoke. "You look very nice tonight, son. Did you just come from a special occasion?"

Josh Whitehall, resplendent in dress khakis, a tan and blue plaid shirt, and a navy sport coat, said, "No, sir. I'm attending a special occasion tonight."

"You are? After you leave? Funeral? Wedding?"

"Right here. Right now. The completion of Daniel's first chemo treatment."

Andy didn't for one minute buy that explanation, aware that another young man would be walking through that same door very soon. Trent had called Faith at four o'clock to say he'd arrived, rented a car, left Logan Airport, and was on his way to Wentworth Cove. It was a two-hour drive, so unless traffic was extremely heavy, he would arrive soon.

"Be there in a minute, Daniel," Josh called. "Let me take this food to the kitchen."

"Here, let me help you with that. You go see Daniel. I'll run this to Em. Josh, you've touched this dad tonight in a way that words can't express. Thank you."

"I'd do anything for him, sir. He's like a—" The words caught in Josh's throat, and his eyes welled with tears. "He's like a brother to me." Josh swallowed and blinked a couple of times, shifted the two large bags of food to Andy, and reserved a small one. "This one's for Daniel. I'll take it to him."

"He's waiting to see you," Andy said, hugging the young man with his free arm and blinking back tears himself.

"Whoa, dude, you're dressed fancy. Hey! What happened to your hair?" Daniel asked as Josh entered the den. "Cool cap! Red Sox!"

"My hair? Who needs hair?"

"But Faith loves your hair!"

"She does? How do you know that?" Josh asked, trying to suppress a smile.

"She told me," Daniel answered, and Josh allowed the smile he'd tried to hold back.

"The good thing about hair is that it'll grow back. I thought it might be fun for us to be bald together."

"Sweet! Are you going somewhere after dinner? What's in the bag?"

"To answer your first question, no. I just felt like dressing up a little for this special occasion. And question number two—something for you."

"Yeah? For me? Why? My birthday's not till—"

"It's not for your birthday. And it's not much. Just something I saw and thought you might like."

"Can I open it now?"

"Sure."

Daniel took the bag, threw tissue paper on the floor, and pulled out a baseball cap exactly like the one Josh had on. "This is so cool! I'm wearing it to school Monday! Everybody thinks I'm a Texas Rangers fan because I'm from Dallas, but I'm not. Well, maybe I used to be, but I'm a Red Sox fan now—just like you." Daniel put on the cap. "We're twins, aren't we?"

"We are, indeed, and we're in this together, buddy." Josh heard a small gasp behind him and turned to see Faith—eyes wide, palms turned up, shoulders shrugged—standing in the doorway.

"What. Happened. To. Your. Hair?" she asked, her voice punctuating each word.

"That seems to be the question of the night. It'll grow back. I just thought it would be fun for my buddy and me to be twins for a while. Turns out he's a Red Sox fan. Who knew?" He reached down and tapped Daniel on the head a couple of times.

Josh looked up. Was Faith crying? She *was* crying. "I always suspected you liked my hair. I just didn't know you liked it *that* much," Josh said, trying to lighten the mood.

"It's not that. It's just that...It's...I've never seen such a demonstration of love," she said as she stepped across the room and threw her arms around him. *Oh, man. I should have done this months ago. If I'd known shaving my head would have sped our relationship along, I'd have—* Josh's thoughts were interrupted by the doorbell, and Faith let go of him. A little too quickly, he thought. She wiped at her eyes and cleared her throat.

"That's probably Trent," she said. "I'll get it."

As Faith walked out, Emily walked in. "What's this I hear about—" Was she going to cry, too? *I'll never understand women,* Josh thought as Emily enveloped him in a hug. "That's about the sweetest thing I've ever seen," she said between sobs.

"Why is everybody crying?" Daniel asked. "It's just hair. It'll grow back. Won't it, Josh?"

"Of course it will, buddy. Mine will and yours will, too. And I'll grow mine back out like it was...since it seems everybody was so crazy about it. Who knew?" And they all three laughed.

"Mom! Dad! Trent's here," Faith called from the living room.

"Excuse me," Emily said. "We'll be ready to eat in a few minutes. Everything's on the table. Thanks again, Josh. You have no idea how much this means to Andy and me."

Faith could feel herself tense up when she introduced Trent and Josh, and the look on Trent's face told her he didn't for one minute think Josh was there solely for Daniel. Dinner conversation stayed light and pleasant, though, everyone sticking to subjects like the weather in both Maine and Texas and how Trent's job at the bank was going.

"What's the deal with the matching ball caps?" Trent asked Faith when Josh had left and Daniel and Landon were upstairs playing video games. "Daniel and the photographer guy? I knew he'd been giving him pointers, but I didn't know they were that close."

What's the deal with guys not being able to say another guy's name? This conversation reminded her of the one with Josh when she told him Trent was coming to Wentworth Cove. What had he called him? The cowboy?

"Do you mean Josh? His name is Josh Whitehall."

"You're awfully fast to defend him. Do I need to be worried? Is Daniel the only one he's close to?"

"What do you mean by that?"

"Nothing. Forget I said it."

"Gladly."

"I don't want to start this visit on a negative note," Trent said. "Let's start over. What's there to do here? Want to go out somewhere?"

"Well…There's really no place to go at this time of night in Wentworth Cove. We'd have to go to Portland, but I can show you this area tomorrow, and we can go to Portland tomorrow night if you want."

"That's fine. I think I'll go to the hotel now and hit the sack early. I have a little gift for Daniel, too, but I think I'll wait until in the morning to give it to him. What time do you want me to pick you up tomorrow?"

"I don't know. How does ten sound?"

"Works for me."

"And Trent?"

"Yeah."

"It's not a hotel, so don't get your hopes up. It is a cozy little inn, though. It's quaint and it's clean."

"Quaint I can believe. That about sums up this place…what I've seen of it so far."

"Didn't you like the ride up I-95? The trees are gorgeous right now."

"They were pretty, Trent conceded. "Lots of fall color. That's one thing we don't have in Dallas. I'll give you that."

"Wear jeans tomorrow, and then we can dress up to go into Portland later."

"Okay. See you in the morning," Trent said, kissing Faith for the first time since he'd arrived. She was glad he hadn't kissed her in front of Josh. She didn't know why, but for some reason she was *very* glad.

"So on a scale of one to ten, how tired are you tonight?" Andy asked his wife as they were getting ready for bed. "It's been a big day."

"I'm fine, really. More emotionally exhausted than anything else. I know Daniel's going to be a very sick little boy soon. And Trent's visit complicated matters. For Faith, at least. She hasn't said anything, but I get the feeling she'd have preferred him to wait and come later, maybe Thanksgiving. I think she'd rather have support from Josh right now, not Trent. Do you think I'm wrong?"

"I feel the same way, Em. Can you believe that guy shaved his head? Have you ever? I mean I've read about people doing that, but I never in a hundred years would've thought—"

"Exactly."

"And he was astute enough to leave right after we ate. If you ask me, he's playing his cards right."

"Is this a game?"

"Kind of. And Faith is the prize. Listen, sweetheart. I know guys, and both of those guys are crazy about our daughter. Who can blame them? She's quite a catch, if I do say so myself. One of them is going to end up getting hurt, and I think Josh has been hurt enough. I don't know much about his past, but that boy's carrying scars from something."

"I know. I feel that, too. He's very sensitive, but he loves both of our children, so I love him. I'd adopt him in a heartbeat."

"You might get him without adopting him," Andy quipped, winking at his wife.

"Maybe. But Faith didn't tell Trent *not* to come, so don't count him out. We'll just have to wait and see how everything plays out."

Chapter Twenty

Saturday dawned cold and crisp…one of those halcyon autumn days that made Faith happy she'd moved to New England. She couldn't put her finger on it exactly, but her feeling this morning was one of optimism. She could visualize Daniel well and herself as a totally happy and fulfilled kindergarten teacher. What part either of two important men in her life right now would possibly play in this she didn't know, but she determined to trust her heart and not worry about the future. To take life as it came. To live one day at a time in gratefulness for the opportunities she'd been given.

Trent arrived at ten o'clock sharp. Daniel was up and feeling rested from a good night's sleep brought on in part by the nausea meds Emily had given him before he went to bed. He and Faith reached the door at the same time.

"Good morning. How'd you sleep? And how do you like this beautiful weather?" Faith asked Trent as Daniel slung the door open wide.

"Why didn't you tell me to bring a winter coat? It's kind of cold for October."

"Oh, man, this is nothing. Wait till you're here for a *really* cold day," Daniel said, playing the part of a proud Maine citizen.

"Hey, Dan. I know you have a Red Sox cap, but I thought you might like a Texas Rangers one, too, since you're from Texas. You like the Rangers, don't you?"

"Oh sure. I like 'em both," Daniel answered diplomatically, refraining from mentioning the fact that no one ever called him *Dan*. "I'll wear one to school Monday and the other one Tuesday. They call me Tex anyway—did Faith tell you that?—so they won't be surprised to see me in a Rangers cap."

"I thought you had to wait till you started losing your hair to wear your caps," Faith said.

"Mr. Cunningham likes me. He won't mind."

One thing about my little brother, Faith thought, *he has an abundance of self-confidence without appearing cocky. On him it's endearing.* "Okay. Just don't get in trouble," she admonished.

"Don't worry about me, Faith. He's cool. Thanks for the cap, Trent. I like it."

"That's great. Hey, would you like to go sightseeing with Faith and me today?"

"I'm a little tired and I don't feel like eating right now, so I think I'll stay home, but thanks."

"Sure. Maybe when you're feeling better," Trent offered.

"Yeah. That might be a while, though."

"Take it easy today, Daniel," Faith said, kissing her brother on the forehead. "Let Mom and Dad wait on you. Don't overdo it. Ready to see the sights of Wentworth Cove and surrounding areas, Trent?"

"Oh, man, I can hardly wait. If it's anything like that inn I stayed at last night, it'll be, uh… interesting."

Back in Wentworth Cove after a full day of sightseeing in Kennebunkport and Portland, Faith and Trent settled in on a camelback sofa in the sitting room at the inn. Trent spoke first. "I've missed you. You know, when I took that job in Dallas, it was partly because I thought you'd be there. I had a better offer in Houston. Did you know that?"

"I thought you didn't like Houston. Humidity and all that. You told me you didn't want to live there."

"An extra twenty thousand a year would have made it more palatable. I'm not sure I would have noticed the humidity. I took the job in Dallas to be close to you."

"I'm sorry, Trent. Are you trying to put me on a guilt trip? Because if you are, you're doing a pretty good job of it."

"I'm just telling the truth, honey. I thought we had a future and it was the next step in our relationship…being in Dallas together…building a life together."

"You knew I wasn't ready to make that kind of commitment. I was honest with you about that."

"Sure. I knew you weren't ready then, but I thought that in time—"

"But I couldn't guarantee anything."

"Okay. Let's don't talk about what might have been. Let's talk about what *can* be in the future." He fished in his pocket and pulled out a black velvet box.

Faith froze. She hadn't expected this…still wasn't ready…didn't know if she would ever be. All day while she'd been with Trent, Josh's face kept popping into her mind. At one time she thought that she and Trent would get married, buy a house in suburbia and two SUVs, and have two or three children. She'd even thought about homeschooling them. But now, well…she couldn't get that stupid crooked grin of Josh's out of her mind.

"Faith, you know you belong in Texas. You've always lived there, always loved it." He slipped off the sofa and dropped to one knee. "I'd thought when I proposed to you, it would be different. We'd be in a nice restaurant in Dallas, candlelight, champagne, the whole bit. But I don't want to wait." He opened the box and revealed a brilliant one- or two-carat—Faith couldn't tell, but it was big—diamond ring. "Faith, I love you. Will you marry me?"

"Oh, Trent—"

"Say yes and let's start making plans to spend the rest of our lives together." He took the ring from the box and started to slip it on her finger.

"No. I—"

"What?"

"No. Don't put it on yet. I mean, it's beautiful...absolutely gorgeous, but—"

"We can change it. I wanted to let you pick it out, but I also wanted to surprise you."

"Well, you *did* surprise me."

"The setting is platinum. I thought you'd like that better than gold, but if you'd—"

"It's not the ring. The ring is perfect."

"It's the photographer guy, isn't it? I saw the way he looked at you last night."

"His name is Josh. The photographer guy's name is Josh."

"You're dating him, aren't you?"

"We've gone out a couple of times."

"Oh, Faith. I know we said we were free to date other people. You got it out of your system. But now it's time to start thinking about settling down. About coming back to Dallas. About spending the rest of your life with someone who can buy you the things you deserve. I've been looking at houses."

"No, Trent. I don't think you understand. I didn't get it out of my system. I enjoyed going out with him."

"And you were going to tell me this *when*?"

"Tomorrow. Before you left. I didn't expect you to propose tonight. This isn't the way I wanted to tell you. I wanted us to just have a pleasant weekend and I'd mention it later."

"*Mention* it? You'd *mention* something so important it's keeping you from saying yes to my proposal? I think that deserves more than a *mention*, don't you?" Trent was having a hard time keeping his voice down.

"That's not what's keeping me from saying yes, Trent. We've been out a couple of times. We're just friends." *Were* they just friends? Or was Faith trying to convince herself? He hadn't kissed her. She'd thought he might a couple of times, but…

"No? Then whatever could it be?"

"I really like it here. I love my job. I'm making a difference in kids' lives. I've established a place at my school. My principal respects me and backs me. I like being close to my parents. And did you *really* think I'd leave Daniel while he's so sick? I don't know how long he's going to take the chemo treatments, but I couldn't leave any time soon."

"I'm willing to wait. A year. Maybe two."

"I can't guarantee I'll want to leave in a year or two. This is where my life is now. I know it's different, and I know it's not your cup of tea, but I love it here."

"So there's nothing—"

"I've enjoyed our time together. I wouldn't change it for anything, but I've changed since we started dating in college. I think we both have in a way. Maybe we've grown apart a little bit. Maybe we would have anyway, whether I'd moved or not."

"Faith, I want you to keep this ring and think about it. If you don't want to put it on by Christmas, you can mail it back to me. Think about what I can give you. I've already been promised a promotion after I've worked there a year. How much do photographers make? What kinds of promotions can they expect in their future?"

"See, Trent. That's the thing. That's it in a nutshell. I'm not going to marry someone because of what he can *give* me. If I marry, it will be for how he cherishes me, how he loves my family, how much he'd sacrifice for me and the people I love. It's about the kind of heart he has. It's about how he makes *my* heart skip a beat when he walks in the room. You're a wonderful guy with so many good qualities, but I can't make myself feel something I don't feel."

"Will you keep the ring until Christmas? Think about it? About what you'd be giving up by staying here? About what we could have together? Think about the fun we had last year."

"Okay. I'll keep it until Christmas if that will make you happy."

"Not totally happy…but a little hopeful maybe."

"It's the best I can do right now."

"Okay. I think I'm going to change my flight to an earlier one and go back in the morning, if that's possible. Maybe I'm hoping absence will make your heart grow fonder, but I may be fooling myself since it doesn't seem to have worked so far."

"Should I cook enough breakfast for Trent? Will he go to church with us?" Emily asked her daughter the next morning.

"No, he's probably already left for Boston by now. I'm going to stay home with Daniel today, so you can go with Dad."

"He's what? I thought he had an evening flight."

"He changed it."

"What happened? Did you break up?"

"Not exactly. But maybe. Sort of."

"If you don't want to talk about it, that's okay. I'm just surprised."

"I don't mind talking about it. I was going to tell you anyway." Emily pulled the small velvet box out of her robe pocket and opened it. "This is what changed his mind."

"Wha—"

"Yeah, right? I didn't expect it either."

"It's *huge*. So what does that mean...that's it's in the box and not on your finger...but you have it? I guess I'm a little confused."

"I'm not ready to be engaged to Trent. Not sure I ever will be. But he wanted me to keep it and think about it until Christmas. So instead of arguing with him, I told him I would. I'll mail it back when the time comes."

"If you don't change your mind . . ."

"I won't, Mom."

"You're sure?"

"I'm sure."

Emily hugged her daughter. "That's good. I didn't think he was the one for you anyway," she said with a smile.

Chapter Twenty-One

Faith and Harvest had agreed to meet Monday afternoon at Faith's favorite coffee shop in Kennebunkport to talk about the article that would appear in *The Maine Way* magazine in a couple of months.

"Thanks for meeting with me, Faith. I'll order for us. Coffee?"

"Sure. Two sugars. No cream. Here. Let me—" Faith said, reaching for her purse.

"I got this. Your turn next time." As Harvest Hansen walked to the counter, Faith thought about how she'd imagined her at first: long straight blond hair topped with a daisy headband, peasant blouse, long flowing skirt, and rope sandals. A girl raised by hippie grandparents would surely be a hippie herself, wouldn't she? But this girl would blend in to any corporate setting. Not at all what Faith had expected, but someone she wanted to get to know better.

"Josh suggested we get together to discuss the best way to slant, well not exactly *slant*, but present this story so it will be to your advantage," Harvest said as she returned to the table and set two steaming mugs down. "He believes in you and your teaching methods, and he's convinced me. I'm not going to make Mrs. Hawkins look bad. I'm just going to highlight the effectiveness of what you're doing…how you're running your classroom. I know when I was in school, I was one of those kids who learned best when I was doing something. When forced to just sit and listen, I had trouble concentrating. I finally realized that I could at least take notes and that would give me a way to focus. Trouble is…I didn't learn that trick until I my high school counselor suggested it."

"Better late than never, huh?"

"True. At least I'd learned it by the time I left for college, and it served me well there."

"I see this as an opportunity, Harvest. Not for me, but for my students and students across the state of Maine. I believe, and hope to be able to prove, that kids who have fun learning will be more successful in school in the early years, on into high school and college, and that their love of learning will follow them throughout their lives."

"I love your passion. Passion I can write about. Passion will resonate with our readers. I'd like to get to know you as a person first, though, what makes you tick. My buddy, Josh, is pretty high on you. You know that, right?"

"We've gone out a couple of times," Faith admitted, wondering what kind of relationship Josh and Harvest *really* had. Was it now or had it ever been more than friendship?

"I've known Josh since he came to work at the magazine three years ago, and I've never seen him like this. We talk a lot, and if you ask me, he's got it bad."

Faith felt herself blushing again, the way she did sometimes when she was with Josh. "He's a great guy. My brother thinks he's the absolute coolest person who ever lived. Have you seen him lately?" Faith asked.

"How lately?"

"Today."

"No. He's been out on assignment all day. Why?"

"He did something incredibly sweet. Did you know my brother has cancer and is taking chemo?"

"Josh told me that. I was so sorry to hear it. I've been praying for him every morning."

"Thank you so much. You'll have to meet him sometime."

"I'd love to. What did Josh do?"

"I don't know if I should wait and let you be surprised or…" Faith said, then reconsidered. "No, I'll just tell you. He cut off all his hair, shaved his head, and bought them matching Red Sox caps."

"He didn't! He cut his gorgeous hair? I can't believe it. But in a way I can. He's a super guy. A little mysterious, but very nice."

"What do you mean by 'mysterious'? Not that I haven't thought that myself…but I'm curious what makes you say it."

"As much as we work together and as much as we chat on assignments, he never mentions his family. I'm always prattling on about my grandparents. I've probably talked his ear off about them, but he's never once mentioned any parents or siblings. Has he to you?"

"He told us his parents are attorneys. My mom asked him if he had any brothers or sisters, and he got very quiet. It seemed almost, well…like he had to think about it. We've never brought up the subject again and neither has he."

"I suppose if and when he wants us to know, he'll tell one of us. Most likely, it will be you. We're just friends, by the way—in case you were wondering. We've never dated. More like a brother/sister/confidant relationship."

"I think Josh said your whole name is Harvest Moon Hansen. Pretty, but unusual. There's a story there?"

"It's kind of long, but I'd love to tell it if you have time."

"All the time in the world. My brother had to leave school at noon today, so I don't have to pick him up. He was too weak from his chemo to stay all day. But he did get to show off his new Red Sox cap this morning."

"Poor little thing. He doesn't know me, but give him a hug for me anyway."

"I will."

"So here's my story in a nutshell. When I was two days old, my parents left the hospital with me, went straight to my mother's parents, said they were going to the store for diapers, and never came back. We haven't heard from them since. I didn't have a name yet, so my grandparents named me Harvest Moon. They adopted me when I was two and gave me their last name, Hansen. When I got older, and kids started making fun of my name, they asked me if I wanted to change it. They said I could pick any girl's name I liked, but I decided to stick with Harvest Moon, sort of in appreciation for them and all they'd done for me, and sort of because I liked standing out. My grandparents say it's made me stronger. They could be right. I'm happy with who I am."

"I love that story. My brother is adopted. He knows and has always been fine with it. Sometimes he tells me he's the Chosen One."

"He sounds like a super kid. I'd like to meet him."

"Sure. You should come over sometime."

"Love to. Hey, do you mind if Josh and I come to your class for a few minutes tomorrow? You can name the time, and I'll see if I can visit Marilyn afterward."

"Why don't you come to my morning class? All those parents signed consent forms. I had a few who refused in my afternoon class."

"What time?"

"Is nine too early? That's when they go into their reading groups."

"Perfect. We'll see you then."

Chapter Twenty-Two

By mid-November, Daniel's treatments had begun to wear down his immune system and he'd been beset by infection after infection. He was now taking his chemotherapy infusions at the hospital in Portland, where he could be given IV antibiotics if necessary. Andy, Emily, Faith, and Josh took turns sitting with him. Emily stayed every weekday and some nights, Andy came when he could get away from Wentworth Cove, Faith stayed on Saturdays, and Josh took Sundays.

One Sunday when Josh was with him, Daniel felt particularly weak. "Josh?"

"Hmmm?"

"Are you still there?" His frailty tore at Josh's heart.

"Sure, buddy. I'm not leaving until your mom gets here in the morning."

"Okay. Good. You know what?" he asked, almost whispering.

"What's that?"

"Remember when you told me about changing light? How it changes when the sun goes down and the moon and stars come out? How it changes in the fall when the sun sets in the different place and the shadows are at a different angle? But there's always some kind of light? It never really goes out completely?"

"Wow. You really *were* listening. Are you a good student or am I a good teacher?"

"Both, I guess. Here's the deal."

"What's the deal?"

"If I tell you something, will you not tell Mom and Dad and Faith?"

"Oh. I'm not sure about that. What if I think it's something they need to know?"

"They don't need to know right now. I just want to tell you."

"Okay. Shoot."

"I think the light is changing."

"The lights in the room?"

"No."

"Outside? The sun? We're in the middle of fall, all right."

"No."

"You have me thoroughly confused then."

"I think the light's gonna change for me soon."

"Still confused. Go ahead."

"Well, you know how you said it never goes out? When the sun goes down, the moon and stars give us light. That's when we used time-lapse photography. Remember when I thought it was *laps*, like running laps? I've learned a lot, haven't I?

"You have. You're the best photography student I've ever had."

"I'm the only one you've ever had. It was kinda easy to be the best."

"You would have been no matter how many others I'd had…But go on. Tell me about how the light is changing."

"Well… It's kind of like the sun's going down and the moon and stars are coming up. I mean, I might go to sleep and wake up somewhere else with a different kind of light, but there will still be light. Just like there's always light here. It's just different. It might even be better. It might be brighter."

"Hey," Josh said, his throat tightening. "How about trying to take another sip of this milkshake?"

"No. Listen. I'm trying to tell you not to be sad. I'll still have light where I am. And I don't want Mom and Dad and Faith to be sad either. Will you tell them about the light? You can explain it to them because you taught me about it."

"Hey. That's not gonna happen, buddy."

"You can't say that. You might not want it to happen, but you're not the one who decides."

"Okay. You listen to me and you listen very closely, because this is the most important thing I will ever tell you. More important than any photography or math lesson I ever give you. Are you listening?"

"Yeah."

Josh's pre-law training made him suddenly aware of Daniel's fragility and the fact that he needed to choose his words carefully. "Here's how I know that's not going to happen. You're going to fight and you're not going to give up. And remember when I shaved off all my hair and I told you we're in this together?"

"Yeah."

"I'm not going to *let* you give up. You know why?"

"No."

"Okay. I'm going to tell you something I've never told anyone else. And I'm going to trust you with this secret, all right? Can you keep a secret?"

"Yeah."

"I might tell them sometime, but I'm not ready right now. I'm telling you so you'll know why I don't want you to give up."

"Okay."

"Daniel, I had a brother one time."

"You did? You never told me. Was he younger, like me?"

"Not that much younger. Two years is all."

"Did he die?"

"Yes."

"And you were sad…"

"I'm still sad."

"How long ago did he die?"

"When he was fifteen and I was seventeen. Six years ago."

"Oh."

"Do you know what I'm trying to tell you?"

"Well…"

"Here it is. When I first met you, I thought you talked a lot."

"I guess I did," Daniel admitted, the slightest hint of a smile appearing on his face.

"At first it kind of got on my nerves, but not for long. You were always so excited about everything."

"I was excited about learning about photography."

"Not just that. You were excited about life. Everything we did…everywhere we went…you were excited about it. And that made me excited. Even if I thought you talked a little too much in the beginning, well…it was contagious, see? Your excitement got me excited. I started really enjoying life for the first time since I lost my brother. And then you became like a brother to me. And, buddy, I'm not gonna lose two brothers. So what I'm saying is this. I'm not giving up on you, and you can't give up, either. I need you to stick around. You hear me?"

"I'm not scared to die, but I don't really want to. I know Mom and Dad and Faith would be sad. Like I would be sad if they died."

"They would. So see why I want you to keep fighting? Not for you, but for me and Faith and your mom and dad."

"Did your brother get sick like me?"

"No. He wasn't sick."

"How did he die?"

"I'll tell you about it later, but I can't right now. Do you understand?"

"Yeah. That's okay. Josh?"

"Yeah, buddy?"

"If I'm not gonna give up, I'd better try to drink some of that milkshake. Would you hand it to me?"

Emily left her house at six o'clock on Monday morning for two reasons. One was to avoid going-to-work traffic, but the most important was to relieve Josh at the hospital. She knew he wouldn't leave Daniel's room until she got there, and he needed to go to work.

They were both asleep when she arrived, Daniel sprawled out on the hospital bed with an arm wrapped around his tattered Boo Bear, the same one that had comforted him when he was three, and Josh leaned back in the recliner in the corner of the room.

Josh awoke as soon as she walked in. "Hey. You're here early," he said, clearing his throat.

"Thought you'd need to go home and shower and change clothes before going to work."

"I do, but I'm not going into the office until this afternoon. I actually have an outdoor assignment this morning."

"Thank you so much for staying yesterday and last night. It's such a help to us, Josh."

"My pleasure, Emily. I probably get more out of my time with Daniel than he does."

"I don't know about that. Did he eat anything yesterday? He hasn't been able to hold anything down lately."

"I went to the cafeteria and got him a chocolate milkshake. He managed to get about half of it down before he went to sleep. Tell him I'll be back to see him soon."

"Sure. Have a good day," Emily said, settling in to the recliner he'd just vacated.

Josh hadn't been gone five minutes when Dr. Layton walked in. Daniel was still asleep, and Emily had started a book, thinking she'd be able to get in a few minutes of pleasure reading before needing to help her son with his schoolwork. So far, with the family and Josh acting as his tutors, he'd been able to keep up with the other students in his grade. Landon, Michael, and Dylan had been faithful to visit him in the hospital on weekends. His principal, basketball coach, and even a couple of his teachers had been by, too. Their visits always lifted his spirits, but he was getting weaker physically. Emily could see it and planned to ask about the possibility of IV nutrition.

"How's our boy today?" Dr. Layton asked. "I didn't get a chance to see him yesterday."

Emily was pleased that Dr. Layton and Daniel had developed the same kind of rapport he'd had with Dr. Cameron. "He's been asleep since I've been here. I'm letting him sleep as much as he can. At least then I know he's not throwing up or hurting."

"Rest is what he needs right now," she agreed. "Is Andy coming this morning? There's something I'd like discuss with you."

"He's not planning to, but if—"

"That's not necessary, but I'd like to get the ball rolling as soon as possible, so I'll speak to you now." Dr. Layton lowered her voice to almost a whisper. "Daniel's going to need a bone marrow transplant. We've had to use some strong drugs to knock out this thing, and they're attacking his marrow. It's what they do—zap the good along with the bad. Normally, I'd advise you to talk with Andy and let me know what you decide, but we don't have a choice. It's something we're going to have to do. I'd like to get you and Andy and Faith tested as soon as possible. We don't have the luxury of time, either."

"Oh, no."

"Don't worry. We can usually find a match in the family," she assured Emily. "It's probably going to be Faith. A sibling is usually the best bet."

"Dr. Layton, Daniel is adopted."

"Adopted? I never entertained that possibility."

"Of course you wouldn't. I actually forget it sometimes myself."

"Is there a way you could contact the biological parents? Do you know if there are siblings?"

"It was an open, private adoption. She was fifteen and would never tell us who the father was. She stayed with us until she delivered, but then she left and didn't want to stay in touch. I know she had been living with her grandparents, but she left their house as soon as they found out she was pregnant and we don't know where she went after the baby was born. I don't even know if she ever married. She'd be twenty-six now, so it's a possibility."

"You don't know anyone who might be able to locate her? We'd have a much better chance of finding a match with a blood relative, preferably a full sibling, but there's a slight possibility with a biological parent."

"Let me talk to Andy. He might have some ideas."

"Ideas about what?" a tiny voice asked. Daniel was beginning to stir, and although they'd been on the other side of the room and kept their voices down, Emily wondered how much he'd heard.

"Just medical stuff. How's my favorite patient feeling this morning?" Dr. Layton asked as she walked to his bedside and began listening to his heart and lungs.

"Okay. Could I have some scrambled eggs…with crackers crumbled up in them? The way you used to fix 'em for me, Mom?"

"They might not be as good as your mom's, but I'm sure our cafeteria would be happy to do that." Dr. Layton walked over to the wall and pushed the red call button.

"May I help you?" a voice crackled from the speaker.

"The patient in 602 would like a couple of scrambled eggs with crackers crumbled up in them." She smiled. "Would you order them from the cafeteria, please?"

"Sure. How's my friend feeling this morning?"

"Well, it seems he got his appetite back," Dr. Layton said.

"Good morning, Daniel. Scrambled eggs, coming right up," the voice from the speaker announced.

"I think I'll step into the hall and make a phone call while you're here, Dr. Layton, if that's okay," Emily said.

"Of course, I'll be here about ten minutes, so take your time. Daniel and I haven't had a good chat in a while, have we?"

Emily walked out into the hallway and dialed her husband's number. "Andy, Dr. Layton says Daniel needs a bone marrow transplant, and she wants us to try to find Jenna. Apparently, we need to do this quickly. Oh, Andy! What are we going to do?"

"First, we're not going to panic. There has to be a way. The FBI locates people all the time, even people who don't want to be found. Of course, she could be married and we don't have an idea what her married name would be."

"We don't have the FBI's resources."

"That's true, but we serve a God who does. The next thing we're going to do is call a family meeting and brainstorm. I'll see if Faith and Josh can meet in the hospital cafeteria this evening. I imagine Josh will want to be in on it, don't you think?"

"I think he'd be hurt if we didn't include him."

"I'll bring Faith, and I'll pack a bag and be prepared to spend the night. You can take her home."

"What would I do without you?"

"Don't ever try to find out, okay?"

"Not to worry," Emily assured her husband. "I should go back to the room. Dr. Layton probably needs to see some other patients, and I'd better strike while the iron is hot with the homework. I think he'll feel more like working now since his appetite seems to have returned. He ordered scrambled eggs for breakfast."

"Well, that's encouraging…after two days without eating anything."

"Definitely. Josh said he drank half a milkshake yesterday, too."

"I imagine if Josh asked him to stand on his head, he'd at least try."

"That's true. See you this evening."

Chapter Twenty-Three

A chill of silence fell over the table as Faith and Josh struggled to take in what Andy had just told them. Josh was the first to speak. "You're all going to get tested soon, right? I know a family member is the best candidate for a bone marrow match. I'd get tested if it would do any good, but—"

"Daniel's adopted, Josh." Faith had found her voice.

"He's what?"

"Adopted."

"We hadn't mentioned it before now because it doesn't make a difference to us, and we knew it wouldn't to you either," Andy said. "But now...well...now, it makes a huge difference."

"His parents...I mean, you're his parents...of course," Josh said, searching for words, "but...you know what I mean."

"Sure. His mother was fifteen and didn't want to keep in touch. So we have no idea where to even start looking."

"We have to find her," Josh said with urgency.

"Do you have any ideas?" Faith asked.

"Actually, I might."

"You might? For real? *What?*"

"I don't want to get your hopes up, but let me do some checking."

"That's the most hope we've had so far, Josh. Bless you." Emily said, enveloping him in a hug.

"It might be a long shot, but a long shot is better than *no* shot, right?" Josh said. "Faith, can I run you home? I have to go to Kennebunkport tonight before I head back to my apartment."

"Well, I was going to ride home with Mom—"

"Go ahead, sweetheart," Emily said. "I'll stay and spend some more time with Dad and Daniel before I go back."

"Okay. If you don't mind driving home alone."

"Not at all. I'll just put the car on autopilot, and it'll take me right to the house. Sometimes I feel like I'm going to wear out the roads between Wentworth Cove and the hospital."

"Do you have time to stop for coffee on the way, or do you need to get back to the house?" Josh asked Faith as they walked to his car.

"I'm in no rush, and I'd love a cup of coffee." They hadn't had much time alone lately, and Faith was happy he wanted to extend their time together.

"There's a place on the way out of town where we can grab a cup and talk. I have to tell you something."

"I hope it's good news...because I don't think I can take any more bad news today."

"It's not good or bad. It's just me being honest with you."

"You haven't been honest with me? About what?"

"Not completely. But I'm about to bare my soul and tell you something I've never told anyone else. I actually told Daniel a little, but not the whole story. And it has to do with my idea about finding his mother. There's a hurdle I have to jump over and it's pretty high, but I think you might be able to help."

"You do know how to pique a girl's curiosity," Faith admitted.

"Well, I could go on letting you think I'm perfect, or… You *do* think I'm perfect, don't you?" he asked with a wink.

"Oh, I do. I do. Please don't tell me something that will change that."

"Not even if it could help Daniel?"

"You're admitting an imperfection, although slight I'm sure, in order to help a little boy you didn't even know until a few months ago?"

"That's what it boils down to."

"He loves you like a brother, you know."

"That's the whole point, Faith. I know he does, and I think the world of him, too. And I've already let one brother die. That can't happen again."

"What do you mean?" Faith stopped in her tracks, and her eyes widened with disbelief.

"I'll explain when we get to the coffee shop," Josh said, opening the car door for Faith.

They rode in silence, arrived at their destination in five minutes, and all the while Faith was racking her brain to figure out what Josh could possibly tell her. He let his brother die? That would explain why he was hesitant to talk about siblings. But she felt like she knew him pretty well, and he wasn't someone who would just stand by and let his brother die if there was something he could do to prevent it.

"Do you remember when your mom asked me if I had any brothers or sisters, and I hesitated? The time you rescued me and took me to the kitchen?" he asked when they were seated and had their coffee.

"The first time you ate with us." Faith remembered it well.

"Yeah. I never knew how to answer that question when people asked, so I always said no. It was easier than going into a full-blown explanation. But now I feel like I need to tell you the whole story so you'll know where I'm coming from and why I need your help to try to help Daniel. I just don't want you to think less of me when you hear this. I guess it's why I haven't told you before now."

"You don't have to worry about that. I know your heart, Josh. I know you're a good person, and nothing you could tell me would change that."

"Well, hold that thought because I might need to remind you of it when I finish."

"Okay. So would you just tell me now? Please?"

"You know I haven't talked to my parents in over a year, right?"

"I figured as much since you never talk about them. I didn't know how long it had been, though."

"There are a couple of reasons. One is because they'll never forgive me for not going into law. They always expected me to join them in the family business. And I was planning to when I first went to Harvard and majored in pre-law, but I always knew, in the back of my mind, that I wasn't cut out for that life. It took me almost the entire four years to admit it to myself…and then another few months to muster the courage to tell them. But the most important reason is that I let my little brother die."

"Josh, what—"

"Let me finish. I'm on a roll, and I might never have the courage to tell you this again, and I have to."

"Go ahead. I'm glad you feel like you can."

"Remember when you said you wanted to go sailing?"

"Yeah."

"I was on my high school's sailing team. I'd just graduated, and Jordan was going to be a junior the next year. We took the boat out as we'd done on many occasions. I knew what I was doing. My parents trusted me. It was a beautiful, sunny day when we left. We went too far out. A squall came up. We couldn't get back to shore in time. The boat turned over. I couldn't find him. I tried, but I couldn't. He could swim, but the wind was too strong. The waves were too high. I kept going down and looking, but I eventually I had to give up. I barely made it to shore myself. The Coast Guard found his body a couple of hours later."

"Oh, Josh. I'm so sorry. And you've had to live with that for all these years. But listen—"

"I know what you're going to tell me."

"No, you don't."

"Maybe not, but I know what all my friends tried to tell me."

"And that was?"

"'Josh, you tried. And you kept trying. That's the important thing.' But it's *not*. The important thing is that I survived and Jordie didn't, and I've had to live with that for all these years. And I'll have to live with it for the rest of my life."

"And your parents blamed you?"

"They said they didn't, but they're not warm and loving like your parents, and it wasn't the same between us after that."

"Here's what I was going to say. Are you listening?"

"Yes," Josh said meekly.

"Forget about your parents for a minute. Would Jordan have tried to save you if the situations had been reversed?"

"I know he would. We were very close."

"What if he hadn't been able to save you? If you were able to look down and know the agony he was going through, would you blame him?"

"Of course not—"

"Well, if he's been looking down at you all these years and seeing the agony you've gone through, how do you think he feels? Do you think he's happy that this has had such a negative impact on your life? Or do you think he'd say, 'Josh, it was an accident. It was out of your control. There's nothing to forgive, but if you think there is, then I forgive you. Now you have to forgive yourself.'"

Tears began to flow freely from Josh's eyes. A release he'd never felt before. Guys weren't supposed to cry. He'd wept at the funeral, but since then he'd managed to keep the tears in check. But for some reason he didn't mind crying in front of Faith. She was soft and gentle, and she understood his sadness. He felt she even shared it with him as her hands reached across the table and clasped his.

In a minute he wiped at his eyes and cleared his throat. "What do I owe you for this counseling session, Dr. Parker?"

"Well, now that you mention it..."

"Yes?"

"You had an idea about how to find Daniel's biological mother...maybe..."

"Can you take the day off tomorrow? Get a substitute and go somewhere with me? I wouldn't ask if it wasn't important."

"I think I could. I haven't missed a day yet this year. But why? Where are we going?"

"We're going to Boston to see my parents."

"Your parents? You and I are going to see your parents? Why?"

"Remember I said that in order to help Daniel I'd have to jump over a high hurdle. I'm going to talk to them for the first time in a year. See them for the first time in over two years."

"How can they help? Don't get me wrong. I'm glad you're going to see them. I think you need to. For you, as well as for them. They've actually lost two sons, you know."

"Yeah. I've thought about that. They're both attorneys and have their own firm. They also keep a private investigator on retainer. I know him. He's a good man and a good investigator. I just have to talk them into letting us use his services to find this woman who gave birth to Daniel and might be able to save his life."

"But why me? Why do you want me to go with you?"

"Because they might turn me down. And because once they meet you and see how much Daniel means to you, they can't say no. They're not *completely* heartless," he added with a grin. "And because having you with me would give me the courage to face them after all these months."

"You make a compelling case. That pre-law degree wasn't wasted after all."

"Maybe you could tell *them* that."

"What do you think the chances are? I'd like to let Mom and Dad know, but I don't want to get their hopes up if you think it's a long shot."

"I think that depends on how much information they have on this woman. This guy is good. I mean, really good, so it's worth our effort. Of course, we have no guarantee that once we find her she'll agree to getting tested. Or if she does, that she'll be a match."

"No. But it's the best thing we can do right now. I'll call Carrie and ask her to get me a sub. What time do you want to leave?"

"I think about eight. That way we'll miss the worst traffic in Boston. And we should plan to head back by three in the afternoon. That'll give us five hours to use your charms to convince them. But your first mission is to rustle up all the info on this woman that you can. Name, age, description, people she lived with, where she might have gone, adoption papers, birth certificate. They wouldn't happen to have a picture of her, would they?"

"I'll see what I can find out and meet you at eight in the morning. Thank you, Josh. This will pay for many counseling sessions."

"Good. Because after tomorrow I might be needing a lot more."

Chapter Twenty-Four

Tuesday dawned cloudy and cold, and a slight dusting of snow covered the ground. Faith had called Carrie the night before and secured a substitute for the day. Not wanting to go into the specific reason for her absence, she'd said only that she needed to take care of something for the family. Her principal couldn't have been more supportive. "Take as much time as you need. We'll be okay here. I have a retired kindergarten teacher who's always willing to fill in. And if you see that you need more than one day, just let me know."

Josh and Faith had told Emily together when she'd gotten home Monday night. Then they'd called Andy at the hospital. "Josh," Andy said, "you'll never know how much your friendship has meant to Daniel. And if you can pull this off, well…"

"I know, sir. I'm going to do everything within my power," Josh had assured him.

Faith poured herself a second cup of coffee and put it in a travel mug before heating two blueberry muffins before Josh arrived. Someone—there'd been so many

Faith had lost track—had brought them with a pot roast dinner a couple of nights ago. Food was still coming in as fast as they could eat it. Faith and Emily hadn't had to do much in the kitchen besides warm up leftovers in months, and Andy's secretary kept them supplied with paper plates and plastic ware, which cut cleanup to a minimum.

Emily had already left for the hospital when Josh arrived. Faith answered the doorbell on the first ring. "I'm ready. Just let me grab my coat."

"Better make it a heavy one. It's supposed to get pretty cold today. What do I smell? Have you been baking?"

"I'll show you when we get in the car. Do you need coffee?"

"No, thanks. Brought it with me. But I *do* need something to go with it," he said, sniffing. "Whatever you have in that bag that smells so good."

"You know how to drive in snow, right?"

Josh laughed. "I *learned* how to drive in snow, Miss Texas. Besides, the snowplows will be out in full force if this gets any worse."

Everyone had told the Parkers it was unusual not to have had a heavy snow yet, but just wait. It would come. And it would probably come with a vengeance. Faith had to admit she sort of looked forward to the first big snow. If it was going to be this cold anyway, she might as well be able to watch beautiful snowflakes falling to and covering the ground. She'd bought snow boots and was ready for a walk along snow-covered trails. She'd actually pictured Josh and her walking together in the park where they'd had their picnic.

Their dates had ended when Daniel started his chemo treatments, each one spending time alone with him and the two of them spending time together with him. She felt she'd gotten to know him even better this way, however. He'd shown her, without overtly trying, the kind of man he was. The way he interacted with Daniel and her parents let her know he was the type of guy she could spend the rest of her life with.

Since the weekend Trent had come to visit, however, he'd seemed to back off. He hadn't asked her out. Hadn't held her hand again. So she wasn't sure he still felt the same way he did when they were dating…before Daniel got so sick. She hadn't told him about the proposal. Now she wondered if she should. For all she knew, he thought she and Trent were still in a serious relationship.

"Dollar for your thoughts," Josh said when they'd traveled several miles in comfortable silence.

"Whoa. That's some serious inflation. I can remember when thoughts weren't worth more than a penny."

"Just color me really curious. Or the last of the big spenders. Take your pick."

"I'll take both…and thank you for offering such a high bid."

"Well?" Josh prompted after a few seconds.

"Well?"

"Are you going to tell me what you've been thinking about for the last fifteen minutes?"

"Are you going to fork over that dollar?"

"Ouch. I thought my credit was good with you. How 'bout I buy you lunch in Boston? I can assure you it'll cost more than a dollar."

"A fair trade."

"So?"

"Okay. Hang on. I'm thinking how I want to phrase it." *Do I tell him the truth…that I was thinking about him? About why we hadn't gone out again? Whether I should tell him about Trent's proposal? Or should I just tell him I was worrying we might never find Jenna with only a name, description, birth certificate, and adoption papers?*

All of those thoughts had crossed her mind, but she opted for the truth. She wanted to know how he would react to the news of a refused proposal. She was curious about *why* he'd distanced himself since Daniel became ill.

"I was thinking about Trent."

"Oh," Josh said quietly.

"And you."

"And me? I was in the same thoughts with the cowboy?"

"You were."

"You're being a little too cryptic for a really nice lunch. So far you haven't earned more than a cup of lukewarm clam chowder."

"Ooohhh. Chowder sounds great on a day like today." The snowfall had ramped up, and Faith enjoyed watching it. It was a dry snow, and Josh's Jeep had four-wheel drive, so she wasn't worried about the road conditions.

"I was hoping to have to pay for a really nice meal at a fancy restaurant with white tablecloths. Lobster maybe? When was the last time you had lobster?"

"On our first date."

"That's too long to go without eating lobster. But you have to earn it. We made a deal."

All right, Faith. Just put it out there. "Okay. I was wondering why you haven't asked me out since that weekend when Trent was here."

"Oh, man. I wasn't expecting that."

"Sorry. If you don't—"

"No, I do. I want to tell you. In fact, I'm glad you asked. The truth is...well, there are two reasons. I didn't want to complicate things with you and the cowboy, and I thought you had enough on your mind. I can assure you it wasn't because I didn't want to. The two dates we had were pretty special. I thought you enjoyed them, too, but then the cowboy came and I didn't know what to think."

"I guess not. I'm sorry if I put you in an uncomfortable spot by not being honest with you."

"What do you mean?"

"I mean...Trent proposed to me that weekend."

Silence. Josh didn't say a word, but when Faith looked over at him, she could read his mind. The look on his face spoke volumes. He thought she'd accepted.

"Are you going to say anything?"

"What's left to say? Congratulations?"

"Congratulations are in order only if one accepts a proposal."

"Huh?"

She held up her left hand. "Do you see a ring on my finger?"

Josh's countenance changed and a huge grin spread across his face. "Why no. No, I do not. I knew that cowboy was too cheap to buy you a nice ring."

"Actually, he bought me a *very* nice ring. But I haven't put it on my finger and I don't plan to."

"Poor guy. I actually feel sorry for him now. Who would've thought *that* would happen?"

"So…about that second reason you haven't asked me out."

"Daniel."

"Yes, Daniel. What do you think he would want?"

"I guess he's made that pretty clear, huh?"

"I know he has to me."

"Weekends are out since you stay with him on Saturday and I stay on Sunday."

"My dad stays with him on Friday night."

"That's true."

"You're out of excuses."

"It seems I am," Josh said, reaching over, taking Faith's hand, and rubbing the place where a ring so easily could have been. "That feels good. A finger without a ring. I won't ask why you turned him down…though I'm more curious than you could ever imagine. But anytime you feel like telling me, I'm willing to listen."

"I will. Someday."

Chapter Twenty-Five

Traffic was unusually light for Boston when Josh and Faith entered the city on I-95. Josh headed downtown toward his parents' law office. He hadn't called ahead, so they weren't expecting him. To be completely honest, he didn't know what he would say to them at first or how they'd respond to his surprise visit. He figured he'd just play it by ear and knew that having Faith by his side, especially now that he was more confident of their relationship, would give him courage to face them. And if he needed even more courage, all he had to do was picture Daniel lying in that hospital bed talking about dying. That conversation sent shivers up his spine whenever he thought about it.

Faith interrupted his thoughts. "Are you ready to see your parents?"

"Not really."

"Anything I can do to make it easier?"

"Just stay by my side and talk when I toss you the ball."

"What should I talk about?"

"Just be yourself. I want you to tell them how much Daniel means to you. They aren't completely heartless.

They can seem like it sometimes, but they're not. Faith, we have to make this work."

"I know. I can't think of another way."

"Neither can I. Believe me, if I could, I wouldn't be here right now."

"Josh, this is the second amazing sacrifice you've made for Daniel."

"Oh yeah? What was the first?"

"Shaving your head. But this is the most important. We have to find Jenna."

"We will. Jack Ryland is good. That's why my parents pay him an exorbitant retainer. He'll be happy to do this for us. The only catch is whether they'll give him the go-ahead. I haven't exactly given them any reasons to lately."

"This is making me homesick...but just a little bit."

"What is?"

"Being in a city."

Josh reached across the seat and squeezed her hand. "Don't get homesick enough to want to go back. I'll get you out of here and back to the beauty of Wentworth Cove as soon as possible."

"Hey, don't rush it. You owe me a big lobster lunch, if you'll recall."

"Yep. A deal's a deal. We're almost there. The first obstacle will be finding a place to park. You haven't lived until you've tried to park in downtown Boston."

"Let me pay for parking. Are there any parking lots or garages that won't be filled at this time of day?"

"I have a better idea," Josh said, whipping out his phone. "Gretchen, it's Josh... I'm good... I know. It's been too long... Hey, I have a question. I'm on my way to the office... No. You heard me right. And I was wondering if I can park in the building garage. Are there any spaces available?... No, they don't know I'm coming... I hope so. We haven't talked in a while, but I guess you know that... Great. I'm looking forward to seeing you. I...actually, *we'll* be there in about ten minutes. I have a friend with me. What number was the parking spot again?... Okay. You'll call Raymond and tell him I'm coming? Are Mom and Dad there?... Well, don't tell her. I want to surprise her. Okay? See you soon. And thanks. Bye."

"My dad's in court. My mom is there. That's probably for the best. We can soften her up and she can soften him up. At least that's the way I *hope* it'll work."

In less than five minutes, Josh pulled into the parking garage beside the building that housed the law offices of Whitehall and Whitehall and spoke to the attendant handing out tickets. "Raymond. How you doin', buddy?"

"I must be seeing things in my old age. Thought I saw a vision of Mr. and Mrs. Whitehall's son, Josh. Couldn't be. He's a hotshot photographer in Maine now. He wouldn't be slummin' in Boston."

"Did Gretchen call you?"

"She did. Good to see you, kiddo. Got number 201 saved for you. On the house."

"Thanks, man. Good to see you, too. Mavis and the kids and grandkids all okay?"

"Fine. Just fine. Got another one since I saw you last. Makes five now. First granddaughter. She won't be spoiled at all." He chuckled.

"Congratulations. I'll see you again on the way out. Thanks for the great spot."

"Any time, my friend. Don't stay away so long next time."

Josh drove the Jeep to the second level and pulled into the space marked 201. "This is good. This way I won't have to clean snow off the windshield before we head back."

"And I won't have to pay for parking... *or* lunch."

"Let's hope the rest of the day goes this well. You ready?"

"I am. Are you? That's the *real* question."

"I should have done this months ago. Having you by my side makes it easier, though."

"I'm glad." Faith smiled at him and squeezed his hand. *I'm right where I belong.*

"Gretchen. So good to see you," Josh said, enveloping the slim, red-haired woman in a bear hug.

"You always gave the best hugs, Josh Whitehall. I've missed those."

"This is Faith Parker, Gretchen Livingstone, the glue that holds Whitehall and Whitehall together."

"I'm happy to meet you," Faith said.

"The pleasure is mine, Miss Parker. Any friend of Josh's is, well, you know the cliché," she said smiling.

"I'll let your mother know you're here. I already told her you were on your way up. Didn't want her to have a coronary. Hope you don't mind, but I have to look out for your parents. They've looked out for me all these years."

"Of course."

Gretchen pushed the intercom button. "He's here. Shall I send him in? And Mrs. Whitehall? He has a friend with him." She looked up at Josh. "Like I said…I look out for her. Didn't want her to be blindsided. That's all."

Josh heard his mother's voice over the intercom for the first time in a year. "Thank you, Gretchen. Send them in."

"Hello, Mother."

"What happened to your hair?" Celeste Whitehall stood ramrod straight behind her desk. Faith thought it was strange that she didn't walk around the desk and hug the son she hadn't seen in such a long time, but as Josh had said, his parents were different from hers.

"I'm gonna get a tattoo on my forehead that says 'It'll grow back.' I shaved my head. For a reason. Mother, this is Faith Parker. Faith, this is my mother, Celeste Whitehall."

"It's nice to meet you, Mrs. Whitehall," Faith said, extending her hand across the desk.

"The pleasure is mine, I'm sure. It's quite an honor to meet a young lady my son brings home after a yearlong absence. Are you from Boston?"

"No, ma'am—"

"Mother, Faith and her family live in Wentworth Cove, right outside Kennebunkport."

"Your family? Husband and children?"

"I live with my parents and younger brother, Mrs. Whitehall."

"She *lives* with *her* parents, Josh, and you can't even come see yours once or twice a year."

"I didn't come here to get into an argument, Mother."

"Then why did you come? Have you reconsidered going to law school? What do you do, Faith?"

"I'm a kindergarten teacher."

"And what do your parents do?"

"Don't turn this into the Spanish Inquisition, Mother. And you wonder why I don't call."

"I didn't wonder. I assumed you were embarrassed about not going to law school after we put you through Harvard."

"I'm not embarrassed about that, but you're embarrassing me now."

"It's okay, Josh. My dad is a minister, Mrs. Whitehall, at the Wentworth Cove Community Church. We're originally from Texas. We moved to Maine in June. Josh and I met when he agreed to give my little brother some photography lessons. My brother has leukemia now and is taking chemo treatments, and that's why Josh shaved his head…so that Daniel wouldn't feel so bad about being bald after he lost his hair from the chemo. He even got them matching ball caps. My brother adores your son."

"Wow. Where did you find this girl, son? I've gotten more information from her in less than a minute than I have from you in two years."

"Daniel is why we're here, Mother."

"I was pretty sure it wasn't to see me," Celeste huffed. "Go on."

"He needs a bone marrow transplant, and as you know, a family member has a much better chance of being a match."

"And I can help you with that *how*?"

"Mrs. Whitehall, my brother is adopted, and we lost track of his biological mother. That's the way she wanted it. It was a private adoption, not through an agency. We need to locate her, and time isn't on our side."

"I see." Celeste relaxed enough to sit down.

"I was hoping you'd let us use Jack," Josh cut in. "We brought some info with us: name, age, description, Daniel's birth certificate and adoption papers."

Celeste Whitehall punched the intercom button on her desk. "Gretchen."

"Yes, Mrs. Whitehall."

"Get Jack on the phone. No, scratch that. Tell him to come up here as soon as possible. If he can't come right now, let me talk to him."

"Okay."

"What kind of a hostess am I? Have a seat, Faith. Josh. Jack's office is one floor down. He should be here in a couple of minutes. I know he's in the building. We were supposed to have a lunch meeting in about an hour to discuss a new case."

"Thank you for this, Mother. How's Dad?"

"You know your father, Josh. He's working himself into an early grave. Nothing I can say or do will make him slow down. His blood pressure is too high. He needs to lose weight. Needs to exercise. But I've given up."

"Gretchen said he's in court. When will he be out?" Josh asked. "We're only here for the day, and I'd like to see him before we leave."

"You would, huh? So you're not here just to use Jack? That's good to know."

"No, I'm not. In fact, I'd like to come back and have a good visit...if you will accept the fact that I have a life in Portland now and I'm not joining the firm."

"What choice do we have? It might surprise you to know that your father got me a subscription to *The Maine Way* for my birthday, so I've been keeping up with your work."

"You're kidding, right?"

"No. I'm not kidding."

"Mrs. Whitehall, your son is a gifted artist and a good person, and he's made a huge difference in the life of an eleven-year-old boy these last few months. I know you're proud of him."

Celeste looked out the window. She didn't try to talk. She couldn't. And Josh couldn't remember the last time he'd seen his mother speechless...or if he *ever* had.

Just then the door flew open and a presence entered the office the likes of which Faith had never seen.

"Well, Josh Whitehall. As I live and breathe. Gretchen told me, but I didn't believe it. How the heck are ya, man?" Josh rose to shake Jack's hand, and the tall, muscled man put Josh in a bear hug and slapped him hard on the back a couple of times.

"Hello, Jack. Been a while, huh?"

"No kidding! And who is this? You gone and got married without tellin' us? I highly approve. Jack Ryland, ma'am," he said, extending his large hand.

"Hi. I'm Faith."

"Well, Faith. You the reason this guy finally showed his face around here? And his head? What happened to your hair?"

"I shaved it."

"Good for you. You up and joined the Marines? I knew you'd wise up one of these days."

"No, I—"

"Jack, Josh and Faith came to ask a favor, and I'm going to ask you to do something for them and treat this as priority one. They need you to find someone."

"Sure thing, Ms. W. There's not a soul on the face of the earth that Jack Ryland can't find. Whatcha got for me in the way of information?"

Josh handed him the folder containing everything they knew about Jenna. He opened it and flipped through the contents. "Um hmm. Um hmm."

"What do you think, Jack?" Josh asked. "Is that enough to go on?"

"Not bad. Good thing I have a contact or two in Texas. Who should I call when I've located the lady in question?"

"Call Josh," Celeste instructed. "Josh, write your number on the folder."

"What time are you leaving Boston to go back to no man's land, Josh?" Jack asked.

"We'd like to be out of here by three at the latest."

"That should give me plenty of time to see if we have any chance of locating her. I should have an answer for you in an hour or two. Good to see ya, man. And you, too, ma'am." And with that Jack charged out of the office brandishing the same boldness with which he'd entered.

"Look, I'd love to stay and visit," Celeste said, "but I'm expecting my next appointment in about five minutes. Are you going to stay long enough to see your father?"

"I don't think I can today, but if it's okay, I'd like to come back later."

"Let us know when you're coming, and I'll have Rosa make those apricot-glazed Cornish hens you used to like. Faith, you'll come back, too, won't you?"

"Well—"

"I'll twist her arm."

"Of course. I'd love to meet your father, Josh. Thank you, Mrs. Whitehall."

"And son?"

"Yes, Mother?"

"Don't wait a year this time."

"I won't. And thank you for letting us use Jack."

"Yes, ma'am. Thank you so much, Mrs. Whitehall," Faith added. "I can't tell you how much my family and I appreciate it."

"Not a problem. Jack needs to do something besides look pretty to earn that hefty retainer. Call me Celeste, please."

"'Call me Celeste'? What kind of a spell did you put on my mother?" Josh asked Faith when they were outside the office. "She's never that informal when she meets someone. In fact, I don't think she ever told any of the girls I dated to call her Celeste. Rosa doesn't even call her Celeste, and she's been with us since I was in the eighth grade."

"I like her, Josh."

"She was on her best behavior today."

"Well, the important thing is that she put the investigator to work immediately. And that means a lot to me. I wonder if he'll be able to find Jenna."

"If she's on the grid at all, he will. He has resources all over the place, and he doesn't mind calling in favors. Hungry?"

"For lobster? Are you kidding?"

Chapter Twenty-Six

Faith and Josh were wiping the last vestiges of garlic butter sauce from the corners of their mouths when Josh's phone rang.

"Josh Whitehall... Hello, Jack. That was fast. I hope you have good news... You did?... Just a minute... Faith, do you have a pen in your purse? Go ahead, Jack... Jenna Robertson... That's her married name?... Do you have a phone number? Address?... Okay. Sure. That'll work great. The Parkers and I really appreciate this, man... Yeah, I know they do... I love them, too. It's just been hard, you know?... I know it has. I won't stay away so long next time... Thanks again. Bye."

"Oh my gosh! I don't believe this," Faith said. "We have a name, a phone number and an address?"

"He'll text everything. The next question is this... What are we going to do with that information once we get it?"

"I'll call my dad. I think he should be the one to get in touch with her. She really bonded with him because he was the first one she told about the pregnancy."

"Here's the text. Let's go somewhere quiet so you can make that phone call."

Josh tossed a fifty on the table and they hurried to the car. Faith's hand was trembling as she punched in the numbers on her phone. "Dad?... No, we're still in Boston. But I have good news... No, I'm not kidding. I have her married name, her phone number, and her address... Yes, really... Just a minute. Do you have a pen? Okay. Josh, hand me your phone. Dad's gonna write everything down and call her right now. And Dad? Will you call us back as soon as you get off the phone...whether you can reach her or not?... I will, Dad. I'll pray as soon as we hang up."

They hadn't been on the road ten minutes when Faith's phone rang. "Dad? Did you reach her?... She what?... Of course. I know you did... I can sort of understand that... Well, we just have to keep praying, right?... No, I won't call Mom. I know you want to tell her in person. We'll be back in a couple of hours... Yes, Josh is a good snow driver, Dad." Faith looked over at Josh and smiled. "I'll tell him, and when we get home, you can tell him yourself... Love you, too."

"She wouldn't get tested? I can't believe that," Josh said. " What kind of person would refuse a request like that? Her own flesh and blood."

"She never told her husband about Daniel, and they have another child now. Dad said to tell you thanks for trying. He knows it wasn't easy for you to go back to Boston."

"We're not finished here, Faith."

"What do you mean?"

"Can you take off another day?"

"Why?"

"Just trust me on this. Can you?"

"I'm sure I can. But why, Josh? If I call Carrie, I feel like I owe her an explanation."

"Tell her you have to go to Texas."

"I must be losing my hearing. I thought I heard you say something about going to Texas."

"Yes, ma'am. You heard me right. We're getting on the next plane to Dallas. I'll get the tickets while you're buying clothes and makeup and whatever else it is that you ladies need for an overnight trip. I'll take you to a store and give you my credit card. Get a small carry-on bag, too. I'll get what I need after I get the plane tickets and make hotel reservations. We'll leave my car at Logan and rent a car when we get to DFW."

"Whoa. Slow down. My head is spinning. Let me get this straight. We're going to see Jenna, and we're leaving on the next plane out of Boston?"

"Yes, ma'am, Miss Scarlet. You heard me right. That's *exactly* what we're doing. It might have been easy to say no to your dad over the phone, but let's see how easy it is to say no to you when you're standing right in front of her pleading for your brother's life…for her son's life. Believe me. If I'd been able to go the extra mile to save my brother, I would have, and I'm not giving up until I exhaust every avenue we have for saving Daniel."

Josh pulled the car off the road at the nearest exit, and they got out to buy some snacks for the trip. Tears streaming down her cheeks, Faith threw her arms around Josh. "Daniel loves you like a brother, you know."

"Just as long as *you* don't love me like a brother," Josh replied, wiping her tears and kissing her hair. "Hey. Dry your eyes. I have phone calls to make and you have clothes to buy."

"I can buy my own plane ticket, Josh. Here's my credit card."

"Let me get the tickets. You can get the hotel rooms."

"We might not need a hotel. I still have friends in Dallas, remember? Let me make a couple of phone calls after I call Carrie about taking another day off."

"That's cool, but I'm not staying with the cowboy. Just so you know."

Faith laughed. "I'm calling Dad's former secretary...from a couple of churches ago...the one who found a scared, pregnant fifteen-year-old girl crying on the steps of the church and took her to Dad's office. She's always loved Daniel and has been an honorary grandmother to him. She and her husband had four kids and never downsized after they all moved out, so she has plenty of spare bedrooms. She'd be mad if she found out we were there and had stayed somewhere else."

"I see what you mean about 'big city,'" Josh said as he and Faith raced toward Dallas from DFW airport. "I expected cows and horses, but all I see are lights and a highway system to rival anything I've ever seen in New York City." He'd asked Faith to drive since she knew her way around, and she was happy to get back behind the wheel in the city she'd left only...what was it? Five months ago? So much had happened. Had it really been only five months?

They'd arrived at DFW at eight o'clock, and Teresa and Larry were expecting them around nine. If traffic continued to cooperate, Faith estimated they would make it before nine-thirty. "What did I tell you? Makes I-95 look like a lonely ribbon of a highway, doesn't it?" Just then they spotted flashing red and blue lights on the side of the highway. "Uh oh. Looks like someone's getting a speeding ticket," Faith said.

"What exactly does a person have to do to get a speeding ticket here?" Josh asked as he watched cars whizzing past them right and left, even though the speedometer on their rental car registered seventy-eight miles per hour.

"Wide open spaces and great roads. No need to poke around."

"I never took you for a *fast* Sunday Girl. Looks like I was wrong," Josh teased.

Faith was glad he was able to keep the conversation light because she was a little worried about tomorrow. They knew Jenna was a stay-at-home mom with a three-year-old. She'd told Andy that much. So they assumed she'd be at home sometime before they had to catch a plane at four. Hoped they could catch her anyway. She knew there were people back home praying.

Back home. It seemed strange to Faith that *back home* was Maine now. In five short months it had become *home* to her, and she wondered just how much Josh Whitehall had contributed to that feeling. Quite a lot if she were being honest with herself. She felt a much greater connection with him than she'd ever felt with Trent. Was it because of Daniel...or would they have connected had Daniel not been a factor? She would probably never know.

"Dollar for your...No. Make that a Tex-Mex lunch for your thoughts," Faith said after they'd been on the road about twenty minutes. "You've *got* to have Tex-Mex at my favorite restaurant while we're here."

"You won't hear an objection from me. If there's food involved, I'm all over it. But I'm sure you've noticed that."

"Pay up then."

"Pay up?"

"Your thoughts?"

"Oh. I was rehearsing my appeal in my head."

"Your appeal?"

"For tomorrow. Jenna's the jury and I'm going to make my final appeal to her. We have one shot at this, Faith, so we have to pull out all the stops. I'm going over all the tactics I learned in my pre-law classes. Mentally preparing what I'm going to say to persuade her to at least get tested."

"I hadn't thought it out that thoroughly. I was just planning to beg and plead. And I'll probably cry...and it won't be for effect. I don't know what I'll do if I lose Daniel."

"You'll know you'd done everything within your power to save him. Just like you finally got it through my thick skull that I'd done everything I could to save Jordan."

"I'm sorry, Josh. I shouldn't have said that. I wasn't thinking."

"I think I'm dealing with it better now," Josh admitted. "Thanks to you. And I think I'm dealing with my parents better now. Thanks to you. They're not perfect. They're not warm and loving and accepting like yours. But it is what it is and I can love them for who they are and not try to make them something they're not."

"That's a healthy way to look at it," Faith said, happy about the way she'd seen Josh mellow over the months.

In a couple of minutes she pulled the car up to a large red brick two-story house in a middle class neighborhood, not old but not new, either. "Here we are...and only fifteen minutes after nine due to my expert driving skills."

"Your *fast* driving skills, you mean," Josh answered, getting out and taking both of their bags out of the back seat.

Teresa met them at the door. "Faith! Oh, how I've missed you and your family! Come in. Come in."

"We've missed you and Larry, too. Thank you so much for letting us stay here at the last minute. Teresa, this is Josh Whitehall, a friend of the family."

"I'm so happy to meet you, Josh," Teresa said. "Larry will be down in a minute. He's putting the final touches on the bedrooms upstairs. He always wants to make sure they're warm enough but not too hot, each one has a bottle of water, fresh towels in the bathrooms, things like that."

"He shouldn't have gone to so much trouble," Josh said. "We're just thankful to have a place to stay. And I'm happy to meet some of the Parkers' Dallas friends."

"Nonsense. He loves it. What else does he have to do since he retired?"

"What else, indeed," Larry said, coming down the stairs. He hugged Faith and shook Josh's hand. "Let's see. Going to the grocery store. Keeping the laundry done. Vacuuming. Shall I go on? You should see the honey-do lists she leaves me every day. *Gentle reminders* she calls them. More like *Crack the whip*."

"Oh hush. You know you'd get bored if I didn't keep you busy. What are we doing to our guests, though? Sit down. Sit down. You must be tired. Have you eaten? We have some fresh barbecue. I could heat it up and make sandwiches."

"Thanks, Teresa. We grabbed a bite at the airport while we were waiting for the rental car. Don't worry about meals for us. We'll eat out tomorrow and have to head back to the airport around two-thirty in the afternoon," Faith said. "I know you'll probably be leaving for work early."

"What if you haven't been able to talk to Jenna by then?" Larry asked. "You're welcome to stay here longer if you need to."

"We appreciate that, but we have to get back to work on Thursday," Faith said.

"Speak for yourself, Faith," Josh spoke up. "I can stay as long as it takes."

Teresa smiled at Josh. "I like this guy, Faith. Josh, you have a bedroom in our house as long as you need it. You could also turn in that rental car and use one of ours if that would help. In fact, we could have picked you up at the airport. I don't know why I didn't think of that when you called."

"How are Emily and Andy dealing with this?" Larry asked. "We haven't kept in touch the way we should have."

"We haven't, Faith," Teresa admitted, "and I don't know why. I never had a better boss than Andy Parker. The two who've been at the church since y'all moved on to that church across town just aren't the same. This new one calls me his administrative assistant. Don't know what that means except that maybe it makes him feel better about giving me more work. I'd just as soon be a secretary again." She threw her head back and laughed.

"Well, I know one thing for sure," Faith said. "Dad would love for you and Larry to move to Maine. He's happy with his secretary, but no one reads his mind the way you could."

"I'm sure you two are tired," Larry said, "and you have a big day ahead of you, so don't feel like you have to stay here and entertain two old folks if you'd rather get to bed early."

"Thanks, Larry. It's been a full day. This trip was unexpected but something we felt we had to do. I know I would like to turn in. Josh can speak for himself."

"I would, too. I really appreciate your Southern hospitality, but we need to get an early start tomorrow if we're going to catch Jenna at home. We might have to make multiple trips to her house, and I don't know how far it is from here."

"I'll GPS it tonight before I go to sleep, Josh," Faith said. "I'll let you know in the morning."

"How about some breakfast in the morning?" Larry offered. "I usually fix it for Teresa anyway. I can just add in another couple of eggs for scrambling."

"We don't want to trouble—" Josh started.

"That would be great. Thanks, Larry," Faith interrupted. "Eggs and toast. That would be wonderful."

"Biscuits okay instead? And gravy? And grits?"

"Yes, sir!" Josh conceded. "I can't wait to get back to Maine and tell everyone at work I was eating a real Southern breakfast while they were having coffee and bagels."

"Great. We usually eat at seven-thirty. Is that too early?"

"Perfect," Faith said.

"I'll show them to their rooms, Larry, while you get the coffee and other things set up for in the morning."

"Yes, ma'am. See what I mean about the honey-do list?" he said, giving his wife a peck on the cheek.

Chapter Twenty-Seven

"I'm nervous, Josh," Faith admitted as she drove toward Jenna's house the next morning. "I didn't sleep much last night."

"Of course you are. This is one of the most important confrontations you'll have in your life. Listen. I have an idea. After the introductions, that is…if she lets us in…why don't you let me talk first. When I say your name in conversation, then you jump in with whatever's on your mind at the time. I think I can read your face, and I hope I'll be able to read Jenna's. We'll be a tag team. Okay?"

"Is that your attorney training coming out?"

"A little bit of that and maybe a little bit of 'Josh intuition.' I'm psychic, remember?"

"I believe you did tell me that. But if that's true, I don't see how you could have missed Trent's proposal and my refusal."

"Maybe the cowboy is just someone I didn't want to think about. Speaking of…"

"Yes?"

"Are you going to try to see him or call him while we're here?"

"Not at all. It was a pretty clean break. I mean, I still have the ring. I promised to keep it until Christmas, but we're not talking much right now, and I have no desire to see him."

"You just gave this David the strength to face a Goliath named Jenna. See. I do know some Bible stories. Bet you thought I didn't."

"No. I had a feeling there were some hiding somewhere and I'd hear about them eventually."

When Faith pulled up in front of 4321 Woodley Avenue, a small white frame house with a neatly kept yard, she killed the engine and said, "Come here."

"What?" Josh gave her a puzzled look.

"Lean over."

As Josh leaned over, Faith gave him the slightest whisper of a kiss. "There. More strength."

"Wow. Just wow. Did I ever mention that I *love* fast Sunday Girls?"

"Not really. But I'm a little psychic, too. Ready?"

"I am *now*. I could fight a hungry bear. Let's go."

Jenna answered the door on the first knock. "Hi, Jenna," Faith said. "Do you remember me?"

"Hello, Faith. Of course I do. I'd know you anywhere. You've grown up, but then I guess we both have, haven't we? You're still as pretty as ever."

"May we come in? This is my friend, Josh Whitehall. Actually, he's a friend of the whole family."

"Well…"

Josh put his hand out, and Jenna gave him her soft, weak one. "Of course. Come in. I can't say this visit is a total surprise. I just didn't expect it this soon. Your dad said you're living in Maine now."

"We flew down from Boston yesterday," Faith said.

"Before you say anything, I need to tell you that I'm married now and I have a little boy. My husband doesn't know about my past...that part of it anyway, and I...I can't do this, Faith."

"Jenna," Josh said, "may I tell you a story?" Jenna said nothing and Josh continued. "When I first met Daniel, I thought he talked too much. I was giving him some photography lessons, and he wanted to know this and he wanted to know that, and before I could answer one question he was asking me another one. But as I got to know him, I learned to appreciate his zest for life. He's excited about everything and he accepts everyone. To know Daniel is to love him."

Jenna twisted uncomfortably in her chair as Josh continued. "When I found out about his leukemia, I was devastated. I hadn't realized how much this little boy had come to mean to me in just a few short months. You see, I had a brother once...and I lost him in a tragic accident. Daniel had become like a brother to me, and his family was kind enough to share him. We spent a lot of time together. We still do. The last time I was with him in the hospital, he talked to me about dying. He wanted me to know he was okay with it. He said he knew his family would miss him but for me to tell them the light wasn't going out for him. He would soon be living in a brighter light."

Jenna's head was down, and tears were falling from her face to her lap. That gave him the push he needed to go on. He was getting to her. He *had* to. This was his final appeal to the jury. "Jenna, I can tell you're a good person. You chose to give Daniel life once, and his life has blessed so many people. Andy and Emily love him as much as if Emily had given birth to him herself. You have no idea how much he means to me. And his sister...well, there's a bond there that you wouldn't believe. I know what it means to lose a brother, and I don't want Faith to go through what I've been through."

Josh looked over at Faith and he wasn't sure she'd be able to pick up the plea, but he'd given her the signal. He'd passed the baton. She cleared her throat, and in a few seconds, found her voice. "Jenna, do you remember when you came to live with us?" she asked quietly.

She wiped at her eyes with the sleeve of her blouse. "Yes."

"Do you remember how my parents told you they would love and care for your baby as if he were their own flesh and blood?"

"Yes."

"Well, they've...we've done that. But we're *not* his own flesh and blood and we can't give him the bone marrow he needs. Josh can't either."

"If I could, I would...in a heartbeat," Josh jumped in.

"But you are. Jenna, I beg you to remember that my parents took you in and cared for you when you were too scared to go back and live with your grandparents. Please do this for them. Please do it for me. Please do it for your son."

Just then a little boy waddled in from the other room wiping sleep from his eyes. "Mommy..."

"Come here, Oliver. Mommy has some friends over. Come sit in my lap."

"He's beautiful, Jenna," Faith said. "He looks just like—"

"Juice, Mommy?"

"In a minute, honey."

"How old is he?" Faith asked.

"He turned three last month."

"That's the age Daniel was when he was first diagnosed with leukemia. You see, we've been through this with him before. He had two years of chemotherapy treatments that made him violently ill. My mother and my dad sat up nights with him, holding his head while he threw up, even when he hadn't eaten anything for days. I know you love this little boy. Oliver, is it?"

"More than life itself."

"Can you imagine losing him?"

"No."

"Then you know how we feel."

Josh felt it was time to jump back in. "Jenna, we're asking you just to get tested. It won't take long, and I'll pay for everything. You might not be a match, but you'll know you've done everything you can to save your son's life. Would you do that for us? For him?"

"Oliver, Mommy will get you some juice now. You sit at the kitchen table until you finish drinking it. Okay?"

"'Kay."

"I'll be right back." Jenna grabbed her son's hand and led him into the kitchen.

Faith and Josh sat in silence while Jenna was in the kitchen, their eyes telling each other what their voices couldn't...that this was a failed mission. Despite their efforts, despite their pleas, Jenna wasn't going to agree to get tested.

"I have another idea. Trust me," Josh whispered before Jenna came back into the living room. Faith nodded.

When she returned, Josh spoke. "Jenna, will you get tested?"

"My husband, Oliver's father, doesn't know. He's a good man, but I haven't told him. I can't tell him, and there's no way I could do that without him finding out."

"Then I have one more question. Will you tell us the name of Daniel's biological father? Maybe we could talk him into it, and—"

"He's dead."

"Are you sure?" Faith asked.

"I'm sure."

"Maybe there are—"

"My grandfather—" Jenna said.

"Wha—"

"My grandfather raped me," The tears began to flow freely again, and as she sobbed, her body shook uncontrollably.

Faith got up, wrapped her arms around this young woman who'd given her the precious gift of a brother, and hugged her tight. Jenna continued to weep in Faith's arms.

"Jenna. We didn't know. We had no idea."

"You were always so kind to me, Faith. Your parents were good to me, better than anyone had ever been. I was happier at your house, even though I was pregnant and didn't know what the future held for me…I was happier at your house than I'd ever been before. I used to imagine what it would be like if you and I were sisters."

"That's why you said you couldn't go back to your grandparents' house. Because your grandfather had—" Faith couldn't bring herself to say it. Could barely stand to think about it. They'd had no idea.

"That and the fact they didn't want me to come back. My grandmother knew, too, and she couldn't stand to look at me. They're both dead now. I found out from an old neighbor."

"And your parents?"

"They were killed in a car wreck when I was seven."

Faith took a deep breath and looked at Josh. "Jenna," he said, "Faith and I are so sorry to hear what you've been through. That's so much more than anyone should have to bear. Do you mind if we let the Parkers know about this when we get home?"

"No. I don't mind. I used to feel like it was my fault somehow, but I know now that I couldn't have done anything to stop him. I tried. He was so strong."

"Of course it wasn't your fault," Faith said. "I'm so sorry you had to shoulder that by yourself for all these years. I know if you told your husband, he'd understand. You said he's a good man."

"Jenna, we're not going to take up any more of your time. You need to see to your son. But if you change your mind, will you let Andy…Reverend Parker…know? Do you still have his number?"

"Yes."

"We still love you, Jenna. Please call us if you need anything. We're not here anymore, but we still have friends who are, and they'll be glad to help if you need anything. You gave us the greatest gift you could ever give us. We'll never be able to repay you for Daniel."

Jenna clung to Faith and cried as Josh headed toward the car.

"Mommy cry?" Faith and Jenna looked down at a puzzled three-year-old.

"Mommy's okay," Jenna told Oliver as she turned Faith loose and picked up her son. "These friends were just leaving, and I'm sad to see them go."

As Faith and Josh drove away, she looked in the rearview mirror. Jenna stood on the sidewalk, holding Oliver and watching as the car disappeared from sight.

Chapter Twenty-Eight

"We did what we could, and I still don't think it's over. Maybe she just needs some time to think about it. She seems like a good person. After all, she chose to give him life once when it couldn't have been easy." Josh tried to console a disheartened Faith as they sat in her favorite Tex-Mex restaurant awaiting their chicken and steak fajitas.

"She's scared to tell her husband. I think that's the only thing holding her back. I can sort of understand that. She's made a good life for herself after all she went through. We had no idea about her grandfather. She did seem frightened of him, but I thought he was angry because she was pregnant. I was ten at the time and not very perceptive about matters like that. I don't think my parents had a clue either. If we had known, we could have—"

"Could have what, Faith? What could you have done for her that you weren't already doing? You gave her a safe place to live and assurance that her child would be loved and cared for. She wouldn't let you do any more. And then when she wanted to have nothing to do with him after the birth…well, I guess what I'm trying to say is this…Your parents gave her her life back. They're the reason she was able to get married, have another son, and make a good life for herself."

"Yeah. That's true."

"What is that great smell?" Josh asked as the waiter approached their table with a platter of sizzling fajitas. "Whoa! Are they still cooking?"

"That's the way they're served. I can't believe you've never had fajitas before."

"Makes us even, then. You'd never had lobster."

"True."

"I guess we have a lot to teach each other."

"I guess we do."

"Could take a long time. I know lots of things you don't," he said, winking at her.

"I have plenty of time."

Josh reached across the table and squeezed her hand. "Hey, you're gonna have to show me what to do with these things."

Faith laughed as she began to teach Josh Whitehall the fine art of fajita-assembling.

The ride back to DFW was a quiet one for Faith and Josh. After lunch she'd driven him by her old house, the two churches her dad had pastored, and the high school she'd attended. She wanted to show him as much about her life before Maine as she could in a short time. Their relationship seemed to have turned a corner in the two days they'd been together in both Boston and Dallas. Some barriers had come down and she felt a thrill of excitement for what the future might hold. For her, Trent was completely out of the picture. Being in Dallas with no desire to see him had solidified that fact in her mind and in her heart. But, although Josh had given her enough affirmation of his feelings for her, she wasn't sure feelings were enough to sustain a lasting relationship. She was looking for something more solid. But was she ready for a commitment?

They were almost to the airport when Faith broke the silence. "It was so hard to call Dad and tell him we couldn't get Jenna to change her mind. And it was hard to hear her talking about what she'd been through. I can't even imagine."

"I know. Listening to her tell about her life put my family situation in a new light. I could have had it a lot worse. A *whole* lot worse."

"I'm so glad you took the first step toward reestablishing a relationship with them."

"Well, we'll see. I need to know they want it, too."

"They do. Trust me. They do."

"And how do you think you know this, ma'am?"

"I'm psychic. Oh. I almost forgot to tell you. Dad did give me some good news when I called him. The Norsworthys started a drive to get people to join the bone marrow donor registry, and so far they have over a hundred names of people who have pledged to get tested."

"That's awesome! I'm signing up as soon as we get back. I might not be able to help Daniel, but there might be somebody out there—"

"Me, too. I wish I'd done it sooner," Faith said as she wheeled in to the rental car area.

Josh had managed to get adjoining seats on the return trip, something that hadn't been possible on the rushed, packed flight from Boston to Dallas, and he was looking forward to four uninterrupted hours of having Faith all to himself. It was the first opportunity they'd had for in-depth conversation in a couple of months, and he planned to take full advantage of it.

"Do you want the window or aisle?" Josh asked.

Faith scooted in first. "It might be a long time until I see my hometown again. I'll watch as it fades out of sight."

"Is that some sort of symbolism?" he asked, happy to be sitting down beside her.

"I guess you could call it that. The longer I'm in Maine, the more it seems like I've been there forever. There's something about it that gets under your skin, I guess. I'll always love Dallas, but it's like a fading memory now."

"I'm crazy impressed with your driving skills, Miss Scarlet."

"I *learned* how to drive on those highways. My dad had me driving on highways before I was sixteen. Of course, there weren't as many of them then. Dallas has changed a lot in the last few years."

"Flight attendants, prepare for takeoff," the captain's voice barked over the speaker.

They buckled their seat belts. "I'm glad I got to see your old stomping grounds, meet some of your friends, and eat at your favorite Tex-Mex place. I just wish I'd been more persuasive with Jenna. Maybe it's a good thing I didn't become a lawyer," Josh said.

"I don't want to hear you talking like that. You gave a great appeal. It would be a huge step for her to admit to her husband that she'd been keeping a secret that big from him for several years."

"It's hard living with secrets, though. I'm glad you know everything about me now."

"I know *everything*? That's no fun."

"Why?"

"What's that legal term attorneys use when they're obtaining information? Discovery? I think the discovery process should be slow, like it's cooking in a crockpot instead of a microwave. The process itself is interesting."

"Then I can draw it out for *years* if you'd like. There's still a *ton* you don't know about me. We can make this *very* interesting," he said, taking her hand in his. "Where do you want to start? My favorite color is red. Is that enough for today?"

"We have four hours. I think we can get past favorite color."

"Not until I know yours."

"It's blue...the color of the ocean and the sky." *And your eyes.*

"Okay. Now that we have colors out of the way we can get to the important stuff. Favorite food? Besides lobster and Tex-Mex. I *know* you love those."

"Food really *is* the important stuff to you, isn't it?"

"It's up there pretty close to the top. Especially anything you and your mom cook."

"So you're a Maine guy who likes good old Southern cuisine. I noticed you were pretty fond of Larry's biscuits and gravy and grits."

"One of the best breakfasts I've ever had. And, by the way, your friends are super nice. I think I'll send them something for letting us stay there. What do you think they'd like from Maine?"

"Well, how about...*no!* I have a better idea. One of your framed prints. They would *love* that."

"I don't want to be presumptuous and—"

"Trust me on this, Josh. I know them and they would really appreciate something personal."

"Done...if you'll help me decide which one."

"That'll be fun."

"Good. What comes after colors and food?"

"I think this is a good time to tell you why I turned down Trent's proposal. I told you I'd let you know someday. Is this 'someday' all right?"

"Absolutely. I'm all ears. Literally, now that I don't have any hair covering them."

"Well, that's one reason. Actually two reasons."

"You decided not to marry him because he doesn't have big ears?"

Faith smiled. "He doesn't make me laugh."

"And all you have to do to laugh is to look at me and my big ears, right?"

"All I have to do to be happy is to look at you and remember that you shaved your head because you care so much about my brother. Trent would *never* have done that."

"It's been kind of fun. Maybe I was ready for a change. I wish I had a full Southern breakfast, though, for every time someone's said, 'What happened to your hair?'"

"You must have a death-by-cholesterol wish."

"Death-by-cholesterol! What a way to go! Okay…so the cowboy doesn't make you laugh and he wouldn't have shaved his head. That's enough in my book, but I have a feeling there's more."

"There's more."

"And that would be?"

"The main reason I couldn't marry Trent…is that I'm not in love with him."

"That's a good one. That's actually my favorite one. Yep. That's *definitely* my favorite." He squeezed her hand and nudged closer to her. "Well, as long as we're being completely honest with each other, I need to tell you something. Something that's been eating at me for a while. I wanted to tell you on our first date, but I didn't want to spoil the mood, and honestly I didn't know how you'd feel about me afterwards. But I need to tell you now because it's been bothering me and I always want to be completely honest with you."

"I can't imagine what it could be. I think I know you pretty well."

"You do know me pretty well now, but when we first met, I was different. I was more self-centered. I thought only of myself…what I wanted…what would make me happy. I hope I've changed…for the better. I think I have. And I think you and your family have been a big part of that."

"My whole family's pretty crazy about you, too."

"The *whole* family?"

"The *whole* family," she said, her brown eyes steady on his blue ones.

"Well, I enter into this confession with much fear and trepidation…but here goes. When Jessica first asked me to give Daniel some pointers on photography, I said no. I didn't really like kids, and I guess the underlying reason was that I didn't want anything reminding me of Jordie."

"I remember you said no at first. But we were so thankful when you changed your mind, and Daniel was so happy. It couldn't have come at a better time for him."

"Do you want to know why I changed my mind?"

"Sure."

"Because of you."

"Me?"

"Yeah. I was pretty taken with you when we met on the deck that day. Do you remember?"

"I remember seeing you, but you were in such a hurry. I didn't know you even paid any attention to me at all. I thought you were just annoyed with Daniel."

"Oh, I paid attention to you, all right. And I was a little annoyed with him at first. But that was before I got to know him."

"He has a way about him, doesn't he?"

"He does, but he's not the reason I changed my mind. Every time I thought about you, I knew I wanted to get to know you. I'm ashamed to say it now, but I used Daniel to get to you. It wasn't right, but as long as we're being honest with each other, I thought I needed to let you know."

"That's it? That's what you were worried about telling me?"

"That's it."

"That's *great* news! I thought you only liked me because of Daniel, at first anyway, and I wondered if you were annoyed that I always had to tag along. I think you've more than made up for *using* him, as you call it. Now I'm worried you're just hanging around for the home-cooked meals," Faith said, smiling at him.

"As much as I love to eat, I can assure you that if gruel was served at your house every night, I'd still think up excuses to come over."

"Good to know," Faith said, putting her head on Josh's shoulder. "I think I'll close my eyes for a few minutes. I didn't sleep much last night."

"Me, too. We'll get home late, and we both have to be up early tomorrow. Sweet dreams," Josh said as he kissed her on the top of her head.

Chapter Twenty-Nine

"Hi, Daddy," Oliver said as he ran to be picked up by his father when Tommy Robertson walked in the front door.

Tommy kissed and cuddled his son before putting him down. "Where's Mommy?"

"Mommy cry," Oliver replied.

"Mommy cried today?"

"Yeah. Friends go bye-bye."

"Jenna," Tommy called. "I'm home."

"I'll be there in a minute," she said from the kitchen. "Putting the finishing touches on supper."

"Smells great."

"Nothing special. Meatloaf and mashed potatoes. I'm coming." She wiped her hands on a kitchen towel.

"Jenna?" Tommy said quizzically when she entered the living room.

"Yes?"

"Did you cry today?"

Jenna looked at her son. Surely he hadn't— "Why do you ask?"

"Oliver outed you. He said you had some friends over. Did they make you cry?"

Jenna wasn't used to having to think this fast on her feet and couldn't come up with a plausible scenario that would explain her tears, so she decided it was time to tell Tommy the truth. The whole truth. Faith and Josh had been right. Nothing was her fault. She saw that now, and her husband would surely understand it.

"Do you want to know before or after we eat?"

"All of a sudden I'm not very hungry. Will it keep?"

"You mean the food? It will keep better than what I have to tell you. It's waited too long already."

Jenna paused, struggling to order her thoughts, then laid it all out before him, holding back nothing. She told him about the rape, about meeting Teresa and being taken to Andy's office, going to stay with them for seven months, and signing the adoption papers that officially made her firstborn theirs. She also told him about Daniel's leukemia, that he needed a bone marrow transplant and had no other living blood relatives. She told him how Andy had called her yesterday and she'd refused. Then how Faith and a friend had come to the house today to try to get her to reconsider.

Tommy remained silent as she talked, let her get it all out, even when she stopped periodically to wipe fresh tears from her eyes. When he was certain she'd told him everything, he got up and went to the couch to sit beside his wife, enveloping her in his arms. "Jenna, I'm going to call Mom and ask her to keep Oliver for a few days."

"Why, Tommy? What's going on?"

"Don't you want me to go with you to Maine? I'd like to be there when you get tested. I've always wanted to see that part of the country anyway."

"You're not mad?"

"Why would I be mad?"

"Because I didn't tell you sooner. Because I didn't tell the Parkers yesterday that I would do it. That was selfish of me, wasn't it?"

"No, silly girl. That's not an easy decision to make. It was easy for me, but I'm not the one who lived it. You are. And you went through all that basically by yourself. Well, you're not by yourself anymore. Do you want to call the Parkers before or after supper?"

"Can't I get tested here? What if I'm not a match?"

"But if you are, shouldn't you be there ready for the next step? I think when it gets serious enough to need a bone marrow transplant, time is a concern. Besides, I'd like to meet the people who were nice enough to take you in when you really needed someone. I'd like to thank them for keeping you safe."

"Okay. If that's what you think is best."

"So do you want to call them now?"

"I want to wait. Let's see if your mom can keep Oliver and let's see how much plane tickets cost. That friend who was with Faith said he'd pay for everything. Maybe we need to call him."

"We have some money stashed away. Why don't you call them tomorrow after we make all the arrangements?"

"Okay. Tommy?"

"Yeah?"

"How did I ever get so lucky?"

"I'm the lucky one, sweetheart. Let's eat. I'm starving."

The minute Faith pulled her car into the school parking lot on Thursday morning she heard the ping of an incoming text. She parked and took her phone out of her purse. *Faith and Marilyn: Will you come to my office as soon as you arrive today? I have something to show you. Carrie.*

Her heart slowed down and she breathed a sigh of relief that it wasn't bad news about Daniel. In fact, she was pretty sure it wasn't bad news at all. Her principal had given her every reason to believe she was valued at the school, and since Harvest had interviewed them both, Marilyn had quit requiring her to sit in on her classes.

"Faith. Wait up," Hannah called as she was entering the building. "How are you? I was worried when you had to take off a second day. Is everything all right with your brother?"

"About the same. I had to make a quick trip to Dallas."

"Wow. It really was a quick trip to Dallas. When did you get back?"

"Late last night. Too late. I have to see Carrie right now, but I'll tell you all about it at lunch."

Faith and Marilyn approached their principal's office at the same time. "Hello, Faith. Have you been sick?"

"I had to take care of some family business. Made a quick trip down to Dallas."

"Oh. You're not moving back, are you?" Marilyn asked.

"Oh, no. I love it here. This is home now," Faith answered and thought she detected a slight look of disappointment on her supervisor's face.

"Come in, you two," Carrie called. "I have something to show you." She held up the December issue of *The Maine Way* magazine. "Harvest dropped these copies by the office late yesterday. She brought one for each of you and one for me. I think her story captures our school's philosophy and your teaching methods perfectly. And the photographs are quite professional looking. I think you know the photographer, don't you, Faith?"

"Yes, he's a friend of the family."

"Well, tell him he put us in a good light, will you? I know you both have to get back to your rooms now, but I wanted to give you these and tell you how much I appreciate your allowing Harvest and her photographer into your classrooms. I know it was a disruption. And Faith…I was wondering if you'd mind presenting some of your teaching methods to our entire faculty at our next in-service day? We're privileged to have you here, and I think we could all benefit from your fresh approach to community learning. Don't you agree, Marilyn?"

Marilyn looked cowed and sputtered, "Y—Yes, of course. I—I'd better get back to my room now," as Faith and Carrie smiled at each other.

Faith was in the middle of lunch and telling Hannah about her trip to Dallas when her phone rang. "It's my dad, Hannah. Sorry."

She stepped into the hall to answer. "Dad? Everything okay?"

"Everything's fine, honey," Andy told his daughter, "but I need you to make sure we have clean linens on the guest bed when you get home today. Could you do that?"

"Of course. Who's coming over?"

"Jenna and Tommy Robertson."

"Wha—What? I thought I just heard you say Jenna's coming."

"You and Josh must have made a compelling case. She told her husband everything as soon as he got home yesterday, and they're coming tomorrow."

"I can't believe this," Faith cried, tears streaming down her cheeks. "Oh, no. I'm ruining my makeup. I really don't care, though. This is crazy! Have you called Josh?"

"No, sweetheart. I thought you might want to do that. You two make quite a team. I'm just saying…"

"Dad!"

"So you want me to call him?" her dad teased.

"No! I will. He's gonna be so surprised. And happy. He'll be *so* happy."

"This is just to get tested, remember. She might not be a match, but Dr. Layton said since Daniel's biological father was in the same family, there's a greater chance. And Faith?"

"Yes?"

"One more thing."

"What?"

"If she's a match, Jenna doesn't want Daniel to know who the donor was. Dr. Layton will tell Daniel a match was found. We have to protect her privacy. Someday she might be okay with it, but not now."

"I understand. And I'll tell Josh."

Chapter Thirty

The flight from Dallas to Boston was a bumpy one for Tommy and Jenna, and Jenna was feeling queasy when she stepped off the plane. She wasn't sure how much of it was the plane ride and how much was nerves. She'd thought about the Parkers a lot these last eleven years…wondered where they were…wondered what her son looked like. They'd named him before she left, so she was able to imagine a little boy named Daniel running around the house, riding a bicycle in the neighborhood, kicking a ball on the school playground. When Oliver was born, she'd held him close and smelled the baby freshness of him and wondered if that's what Daniel had smelled like when Emily held him.

In a way, this would be closure for her. Even though she wouldn't see Daniel, she would see where he lived, where he rode his bicycle, where he did his homework. That would be enough for her. To know he was happy and to know she had given him a second chance at life. *Please let me be a match*, she prayed. *I believe you led me to those church steps for a reason, so let me help this child of yours continue to bless the Parker family.*

"Do you feel any better?" Tommy asked as he approached with their luggage.

"A little. I think I'm mostly nervous about seeing Andy and Emily again. Feeling a little guilty for not wanting to keep in touch when they really wanted to."

"If they're the kind of people you say they are, I'm sure they understand. You gave them a precious gift, after all." Tommy put his arm around his wife, reached down and kissed her forehead. "We'd better go. Andy's probably waiting for us outside."

Andy picked up his phone on the first ring. "Reverend Parker? Janine Layton here with good news. We have a match."

He'd driven Tommy and Jenna to Dr. Layton's office in Portland the morning after their arrival for a cheek swab, a blood test, a physical exam, and a questionnaire. The results from the swab and blood test were back faster than he expected. Apparently, Dr. Layton had some pull in the hospital lab. "Fantastic news! I can't wait to tell Emily…and Jenna. Jenna's been really nervous about this."

"She's a brave young lady who's been through a lot already. She deserves some good news. I'm calling in a team from Boston and will schedule the procedure as soon as possible. You go spread this happiness to your family, and I'll put Carol to work scheduling everything. Daniel's eating better now, so his body should be ready in about five days. We'll do some more prep work on Jenna during that time. She's staying with your family, right?"

"She and her husband. He's been very supportive."

"Good. Okay if I contact her through you?"

"Perfect. And Dr. Layton?"

"Yes?"

"Emily and I can't thank you enough for your hard work and support through all of this."

"My pleasure, Reverend. I've grown rather fond of that son of yours. He's a trip…even when he's not feeling up to par. Always has a good attitude."

Since their arrival in Wentworth Cove, Jenna and Tommy had kept themselves occupied helping out around the house as best they could. Jenna did some cooking and some deep cleaning that Emily had had to let go for several months. Tommy constantly looked for projects…things that needed to be repaired. So far he'd fixed an electric can opener, sharpened a drawer full of kitchen knives, and trimmed some tree limbs that were in danger of breaking in the next heavy snow.

"You know I need to get back to work in a couple of days. Will you be okay staying here and going through the transplant without me?" Tommy asked his wife one day when they were both working in the Parkers' kitchen.

"I'll be fine. You do what you need to do. I know Oliver wonders where we are. It'll be good for him to see you, and you can tell him I'll be—"

"Was that someone at the door?" Tommy interrupted her.

"Sounded like it. Would you get it? I'm up to my elbows in flour."

"Will do."

Tommy flung open the living room door. "Josh. Come in. Didn't know you were coming over today. Jenna, it's Josh," he called. "She's cooking up something. Faith and Emily will be home soon, and she wants to have dinner ready when they get here. Andy's spending the night at the hospital."

Josh followed Tommy into the kitchen. "Something smells so good. Let me guess. You're making something with flour, am I right?"

"How could you tell?"

"I'm psychic…as Faith can testify."

"Will you stay and eat with us?" Jenna asked.

"Only if you twist my arm. That is, if there's enough."

"I'm making several chicken pot pies so they'll have some in the freezer after I leave. So yeah. There's enough."

"I'd love to. I came to see Faith, but I wanted to talk to you, too, Tommy."

"Yeah? Shoot."

"I know you said you could stay only a few days, and I have to go to Boston this week, so I was wondering if you're planning to fly back anytime soon. If you are, maybe we could sync our schedules and save Andy a trip to the airport."

"I was just telling Jenna I need to get back. Let me fire up the computer and see when I can get a flight. I know Andy's been burning the candle at both ends. I was thinking about taking the bus, but a ride would be great. Want to set the table while I check flights?"

"Sure. I can handle that. How many are eating? Five?" Josh asked, gathering napkins and silverware. "You know what, Jenna?"

"What's that?"

"I'll bet if we could turn back the clock to June, you and I are the last two people the Parkers would have expected to be taking over kitchen duties in their home. So much has happened since they moved here. To them. To me."

"To me," Jenna agreed.

"You know how some people rescue stray animals? They do that with people. At least that's what they did with me. Took me right in and made me a part of their family when I most needed it."

"Oh my goodness. I know what you're talking about. I was just a scared fifteen-year-old girl sitting on the steps of a church wondering what to do next. Wondering how to have an abortion but too embarrassed to tell anyone I was pregnant. Then Teresa walked out the front door, and my life changed."

"Have you seen Teresa since Daniel was born?"

"Once. She came to visit me in the hospital, but I didn't want to see anyone after I left. I wasn't thinking straight."

"You should call her when you get back to Dallas. I know she'd love to see you and meet Tommy and Oliver. She and her husband are nice. We stayed with them when we were down there. Larry makes the best breakfast on the face of the earth. Yeah. You really should call her."

"I might. No guarantees."

Tommy called from the next room, "I can get on a one o'clock flight day after tomorrow. Will that be convenient for you, Josh?"

"Works for me. I can get you to the airport around eleven-thirty and then have lunch with my parents. I'm trying to mend some fences."

"I need to do some of that when I get back to Dallas, too," Jenna said. "There are some people I haven't been completely honest with. Finding Daniel—or rather you finding me—has been the first step on my road to healing. It's been good to reconnect with the Parkers. And as much as I'd love to meet my firstborn, I don't think this is the right time...for him or for me. Maybe when he's older—and well—and I'm not as raw emotionally. In the meantime, Emily is going to send pictures and reports on how he's doing. I didn't want it at first, but I do now. I realize that no matter how hard I tried to rid myself of the memory of giving birth to a son when I was fifteen, I could never forget him. I feel healthier emotionally now. I think I'm on the road to recovery. Thank you, Josh, for the part you played in that. For not giving up on finding me.

For not accepting that I wouldn't consider the bone marrow donation. For making yourself vulnerable enough to tell me about your brother. I know that wasn't easy for you, but it made all the difference in the world to me."

"To me, too, Josh," Tommy said, entering the kitchen with a printed airline ticket in his hand. "I always felt like there was an underlying sadness about Jenna, and now I know it was caused not only by what happened to her, but by living with the secret. I don't think Daniel is the only one who will heal from this transplant."

Chapter Thirty-One

Late autumn morphed into winter—maybe not by the calendar, but by the temperature—and Daniel gained strength with each passing day. The bone marrow he'd received from Jenna—just a kind donor, they'd told him—had given him the boost he needed to tolerate the chemo he was still taking, now as an outpatient. He was happy to be back home and able to attend school one or two days a week.

"Hey, Faith," he said to his sister one day when she picked him up from school, "Josh is a great guy, isn't he?"

"Yeah, buddy. He's a really great guy."

"I like him better than Trent."

"No kidding? I never would have guessed that."

"Do you?"

"Yes, Daniel, I do. I like him a lot better than Trent."

"Do you still have that ring Trent gave you?"

"Yes. Why?"

"I was just wondering. I think Josh would be glad if you sent it back."

"Has he said something to you about it?"

"No. He didn't say he would. I just think he would."

"I told Trent I'd keep it until Christmas."

"It'll be Christmas pretty soon," he said, making his sister smile as he so often did.

The more Faith thought about her brother's words, the more she realized it *would* be Christmas soon. Knowing the ring would never have a home on her finger, she figured it might as well head back to Texas a little early. Although they didn't talk much anymore, she considered Trent a friend and didn't want to lead him on. The sooner she made their break official, the sooner he could get on with his life. She hoped he would start dating other girls. Right now, she suspected his false hopes were standing in the way of his finding someone else.

No time like the present. She and Josh were going Christmas shopping and to dinner afterwards, and the ring would be out of the picture by the time he picked her up.

She felt a renewed excitement as she pulled on a wool sweater over her plaid shirt. Layering, she'd learned, was the key to enjoying a Wentworth Cove winter. That, along with the joy of watching a soft, quiet snowfall with flakes as big as dimes. She couldn't claim proficiency at driving in it yet, but she was getting there…with the help of her new driving coach. Josh had been letting her take the wheel when they were together. After all, he'd told her, anyone who could maneuver Dallas freeways as expertly as she had should have no trouble with a little snow.

"Where are you going?" Daniel called as she donned her jacket and headed for the front door.

"To the post office," she answered, holding up a small box and smiling.

"Can I go with you?" Daniel's energy level was slowly coming back since he'd come home from the hospital.

"Sure. Grab your coat."

"Sweet!"

"Mom! Daniel's running an errand with me," Faith called toward the kitchen.

"Grab your coat, Daniel!" his mother called back.

Daniel grimaced. "Is there an echo in here?" he whispered to Faith.

"Hey, buddy, you're lucky to have two women who love you so much and look out for your best interest," Faith reminded him.

"Yeah, I know. But I'm almost grown. I can remember my coat when it's this cold."

"I don't know about 'almost grown,' but you do have a point about the coat," his sister conceded.

"Did you know I saw my father when I took Tommy to the airport?" Josh asked Faith when they'd finished their dinner at Bay Street Restaurant in Kennebunkport after an afternoon of Christmas shopping. He took her hand as they walked toward the car.

"I thought maybe you did. How did it go?" she asked.

"I guess as good as I could have expected after not seeing or talking to them for over a year. He didn't hug me, but he did shake my hand. So that's a start, right?"

"Of course it is. I'm proud of you for making the effort to go see him. I know it wasn't easy."

"So I've been talking to my mother, too. She wants me to come home for Christmas."

"You have to go, Josh," she said, stopping in the middle of the sidewalk.

"I told her I'd come for Christmas dinner. They have it at seven on Christmas Day. Your mom already invited me for Christmas dinner at your house, but she said we'll eat at one. Are you up for two big meals on one day?"

"Are you sure I'm invited?"

"Absolutely. *Celeste* said, and I quote, 'Please bring Faith so I can get more information on what you've been doing for the last year.'"

"And what did you say?"

"I said, 'I'll issue the invitation and let you know.'"

"I'd be happy to go with you."

He planted a kiss on her forehead. "Whew! Everything's so much easier with you by my side."

"I'd like to get to know your parents better. Oh. By the way, I mailed the ring back to Trent today."

"I know," Josh said with a twinkle in his eye.

"What? How do you know?"

"How do you think?"

"Daniel!"

"He called me. Couldn't wait to tell me. Almost tripped over his tongue he was talking so fast."

"A girl can't have any secrets anymore, I guess."

"I guess not," he said and kissed her again. "A guy can, though."

"You have a secret?"

"I do."

"Are you going to let me in on it…or do I have to find out from my little brother?"

"I didn't tell Daniel. How do you think I kept it a secret? I love the kid, but I don't trust him with my secrets."

"So? Are you gonna make me beg?"

Josh maneuvered Faith to a bench on the outskirts of the parking lot.

"You might want to be sitting down for this."

Faith sat, her eyebrows raised, her shoulders shrugged.

"What's so—"

"I was going to wait until Christmas Eve," he said, "but I went shopping by myself earlier today and, well…I can't wait." Josh dropped to one knee. Faith's eyes widened and her throat tightened. He reached into his coat pocket and pulled out a small black velvet box, similar to the one

Trent had produced a few weeks earlier...and yet...so different.

"Faith Parker, I'll admit to being drawn to your outer beauty at first, but as I got to know you, I saw a beauty on the inside that I'd never known in anyone else. I'm a better person when I'm with you, and I've fallen helplessly, hopelessly in love with you. Will you do me the honor of making me the happiest and most thankful man on the face of the earth and begin the 'discovery' process with me...the one that will take a lifetime? Will you marry me?"

Faith's heart beat hard and fast in her chest, and she took a slow, deep breath to regain control. Not that she hadn't thought about this moment...many times, in fact. She knew how Josh felt about her. He'd let her know in so many ways. But she hadn't expected it so soon, not tonight for sure. She was, however, sure about her feelings for him. She knew there would never be anyone she could love and respect more than she loved and respected this man who was kneeling before her with an open ring box.

"Josh Whitehall," she said, placing her soft hands on his broad shoulders, "I'll admit to being attracted to your appearance at first, too. In fact, when you walk into the room, my heart still skips a beat when I look into your eyes. And at first I thought you were a little standoffish, but when I got to know the real you...the guy who grew to love not only me but my whole family...I knew I could never be satisfied with anyone else. I'm ready to start the 'discovery' process with you...to spend the rest of my life getting to know you and loving you. So *yes*! Yes, I'll marry you!"

Slowly, and with almost a reverence, he removed the ring from the box and slipped it on her finger. "If you'd like a different style, we can change it. Don't be afraid to let me know. I just want you to be happy."

"I love it, Josh. I could never love a ring the way I love this one. It's *perfect*. It's *beautiful*. And I can't wait to show it to everyone."

"Let's go back to your house then. I have an Italian cream cake in the back of the Jeep. I know it's one of Daniel's favorites. I thought we could tell your parents together. It's customary to ask for their blessing *before* the proposal, though, isn't it? Guess I kind of got it backwards."

"You had their blessing *months* ago. But you *were* kind of presumptuous to buy the celebration cake. What made you so sure I'd say 'yes'?"

"I'm psychic," he said, standing and pulling her up into his arms. He hugged her so hard she could barely breathe. But as he released her slightly, his kiss was as soft as the snow that was beginning to fall, and Faith was sure she could spend a lifetime wrapped in his warm embrace.

About the Author

Rebecca Stevenson is a freelance editor and writer whose frequent visits to New England have become the inspirations and settings for her stories. She is a member of Romance Writers of America and Dallas Area Romance Authors and currently lives in Texas with her husband.

Website

http://www.rebeccastevensonwriter.com